Finally the Women Sing

Short Stories
by
Sue Gale

First published in paperback by
Michael Terence Publishing in 2024
www.mtp.agency

ISBN 9781800947528

Cover image
by Greg Williams

Michael Terence
Publishing

Contents

A Little Talk with Jesus

Effie's husband Tom, alongside Rose Netherstreet and a man they have just met in the pub, are in bed together in Rose's flat when a rogue bomb explodes and kills them instantly. Effie hears the blast as she cycles home from work and stops. Her heart flutters slightly as it had done during the Blitz, but then she continues on her way.

'Alright Effie?' Bridget says later that day. She is wearing a cheap woollen headscarf which cannot contain her thick curly hair, and some petroleum jelly on her lips which make them shine. The purple sky is heavy and Effie smiles briefly. She shuffles into the group of women huddled together at the bus stop, their heads bowed beneath a sudden icy-sharp shower. Plastic rain hats are tied beneath chins to protect the grey sculpted waves released from metal curlers that morning.

It is cold but comforting standing there in this post-war weary winter. Effie, Bridget, and the other women are on their way to the Women's Bright Hour meeting at Drummond Road Church Hall, a meeting which purports to provide 'A Beacon of Light through God's Word, for Those in Despair.' The religious element has little appeal for Effie but since she received the letter that morning she certainly feels in despair.

It lies in Effie's pocket. She would have preferred the official brown envelope from the War Office, those harbingers of dread for so many during the war. Instead, she has this grubby grey envelope, her name and address written on it in Tom's careful, child-like hand.

Alighting from the bus at Southwark Park, bare spindly cherry trees mark their way as they trudge through muddy puddles and potholes. Effie is glad of Tom's galoshes even though they are far too big. The church hall stands next to a bomb site where children are playing in a deep crater, building camps from twisted iron girders, and creating their own furniture using old bricks and lumps of splintered wood. The hall itself is miraculously undamaged and stands awkwardly alone between hastily erected prefabricated huts, temporary shelter for those whose homes are in ruins under the mountain of rubble.

An aroma of lavender and camphor meets Effie and Bridget as they go inside the hall. Gentle steam rises from the damp threadbare coats and mackintoshes which hang on a row of crooked pegs by the door. Effie removes her hat and coat and makes her way into the main hall where women are scuttling about meeting and greeting. She sits down on one of the wooden chairs deliberately designed to be uncomfortable, a penance for the sinners who sit there she supposes. Bridget slips in beside her and offers her a peppermint.

'Bloody parky in here,' she says. They move closer together and laugh.

'No Connie?' says Bridget looking around. 'It must be Visiting Day. Poor bleeder. Can't be much fun visiting that bastard on a day like today.' Effie does not reply.

Conversation reduces to a buzzing murmur when the vicar's wife, wearing an unfortunate red beret, stands up. She is at least twenty years younger than most of the women there and they make sure she never forgets it, constantly reminding her of her good fortune; she has a husband who still receives a wage, albeit a meagre one, and who does not imbibe alcohol. Or so they believe.

'Good afternoon, ladies,' she says, unaware that the remains of her lunch are clearly visible down the front of her cardigan. Effie's heart sinks. The vicar's wife delivers the afternoon's sermon in a barely audible monotone. Her well-intentioned platitudes have been heard many times before but as she speaks there are grunts of approval and cries of 'Amen' from those who are listening as well as from those, like

Bridget quietly manicuring her nails, who are not. These afternoons have little to do with spiritual guidance although perhaps they are not so far removed from worship. The women enjoy the singing, their trembling voices battling gamely with a badly tuned piano. A favourite hymn is 'A Little Talk with Jesus.' Written for children, it has a rollicking rhythm not dissimilar to the singsong they are all familiar with at The Blue Anchor on a drunken Saturday night. As they sing the old building creaks uneasily.

At the end of the service, Bridget sighs with relief and unexpectedly takes Effie's hand. There is a quickening in the air. The women stand and stretch tired limbs and bent backs with renewed energy. Arthritic fingers fumble with the strings of shabby cotton overalls. Tarnished silver urns appear from nowhere, and strong brown tea is poured into thick white church-china cups.

Bridget has not brought her usual home-made sponge which uses most of her powdered egg for the week and nearly all her sugar ration. Instead, she has cooked up a batch of coconut pyramids with a precious tin of evaporated milk, some pre-war dried coconut she discovered at the back of the cupboard, and a tiny bottle of cochineal. It is party food, and the little bright pink hillocks look incongruous amidst the stale rock buns and seed cake the other women have struggled to produce in their dark, dank sculleries.

'Tea, Effie?' calls Bridget from the front of the queue. She brings two cups. Effie spills a little on the arm of her chair and scrubs at the small puddle with her handkerchief.

Rickety card tables of varying heights are being erected around the hall. Sheets of cheap brown paper and stubby pencils are delivered to each one. A ground swell of fresh delight greets the arrival of chipped eggcups, a small red dice nestling inside each one. Effie can almost see Tom's expression now, sneering and mocking the women's palpable enjoyment of a Beetle Drive. But Tom has not been home for several days, and she forces herself to concentrate on the chatter and gossip around her. The hissing urns, the chink of cheap crockery, the smells of rancid butter and rubber boots drying in the draughty hallway, provide a security she rarely feels at home with Tom. The two of them sitting together in silence. Just the two of them. Waiting.

Silence descends. Effie and Bridget sit side by side as The Beetle Drive begins in an atmosphere of almost unbearable tension. Gnarled old hands rattle the eggcups, whispering and entreating: 'A six *please*, a five, a leg, a tail is all I ask of you Lord Jesus.' Old hearts, dependent on the fall of the clattering dice, thump. There are sighs of frustration as crooked drawings of beetles' bodies and limbs are scrawled on to the sheets of paper. Effie is surprised at how seriously Bridget is taking the game because when a frail voice cries out in the gloom 'Beetle!' she cries out too in genuine disappointment. Effie takes her hand this time but does not look at her.

Eyes full of confusion, Mrs Sailor the butcher's wife stares down sadly at her alarming beetle – three bodies, two heads, a tail but only one leg. She is reputed to be suffering from shell shock (though heaven knows, whispers Bridget to Effie, Billericay was hardly on the frontline.) The suspect practices of Mr Sailor during the war have made Mrs Sailor unpopular and some say her mental state is a punishment from God for abandoning the docklands of Bermondsey in 1943 for the rural bliss of Essex.

At the end, Effie watches as aprons are removed, carefully folded, and tucked into shopping bags. Coats, hats, and waterproof shoes are put on again. She is sorry the afternoon is over. Outside the rain is now an invasive drizzle, and she marches arm in arm with Bridget through bomb-scarred streets, through the park, back to the bus stop. Their galoshes squelch as they stride across cracked pavements but now, they are laughing - full of warmth, sugar, and God.

Effie boards the bus. Tom's letter has gained weight in her coat pocket and appears to be causing the material to sag. She knows what it will say. Frankly, Rose Netherstreet is welcome to him. She doesn't care anymore. She wonders if Rose will ever have to creep out to women's meetings without Tom's knowledge, if Rose will put up with the back of his hand if there is no hot meal on the table seconds after he returns from The Blue Anchor, if Rose will spend days agonising, praying her monthly wouldn't arrive?

Effie puts her coat away in the heavy oak wardrobe which belonged to Tom's mother, and which blocks out any natural light in the bedroom. In future she decides she will wear her best wedding/funeral coat for 'every day.' Although the cuffs are frayed and she may have to take the hem down again, it has a few years of wear left in it yet. Tom says the tiny sliver of fur on the collar makes her look like a whore, but quite what he means by that she does not know. There were certain women her mother would look at and say, 'she'll not go up the aisle in white,' and Effie supposes they are the ones to whom Tom is referring.

She stares at herself in the mirror. Her hair needs cutting, her skin is pallid, and her eyes are red, disappearing into the heavy folds of flesh above and below them. Creases around her mouth have deepened but the pressure of recent days is lessening. Tom has still not come home but she can forget the suspicions and anxieties of her marriage when she is at The Bright Hour because she knows she is with others who would sympathise if she could ever pluck up the courage to tell them. It is not just the Bright Hour which has cheered her; she has a pleasant feeling in the pit of her stomach whenever she thinks of Bridget.

'Jesus Christ,' she thinks. 'What's wrong with me?' She stares up at the sodden sky through the scullery window. Quite suddenly she recalls a conversation she had with her mother several years before she married Tom. She had asked in all innocence what a lesbian was. Her mother had looked up sharply from her knitting.

'Where have you heard that word?' she said.

'At work.' Effie wished she had not mentioned it and looked down at her darning. Her mother clearly felt some explanation was required. It was rare for Effie to ask her anything.

'It's when, well, when a woman is fond of another woman.'

'So, am I one?' said Effie. 'I'm fond of a lot of women.'

'No.' Her mother's tone was quietly aggressive. 'Not that sort of fond. It's like a man and a woman fond.'

Effie was silent.

'Do you mean they…interfere with each other?'

'I think I've said quite enough.' Her mother stood. 'They didn't have them in my day so I can't say more than that.'

Just then Effie becomes aware of a loud banging at the front door. She hurries downstairs to open it and finds two policemen on the doorstep, awkwardly looking down at their boots.

'Mrs Lawrence? Effie Lawrence?' Effie stares at them. They look uncomfortable. She stands aside to let them into the gloomy hallway which rarely sees the light of day. The older policeman speaks first. He is sombre, and his downturned mouth and sympathetic frown suggest he is practiced at delivering bad news.

'It's your husband Tom, Mrs Lawrence. There's been a terrible accident and I'm afraid he was one of three people killed this morning in a bomb blast in Evelyn Street.'

'Killed?' says Effie. 'He can't have been…'

'Yes, a bomb. German, I reckon…' The younger policeman speaks with inappropriate enthusiasm. 'Bad luck for it to go off two years after we beat the bastards…' The older policeman cuts in quickly.

'We are very sorry Mrs Lawrence. We have the paperwork and some of his things at the station if you want to collect them. His wallet, a ring…'

'A ring? Tom never wore a ring. You sure you got the right man?'

'Oh yes,' says the young policeman. 'Insurance number in his wallet. I had to check it out.' He looks at her to ensure she understands the weight of this responsibility.

'Would you like us to walk with you to the station now and we can sort out the details?' The older policeman speaks kindly but is keen to get away.

'Details?' Effie feels at a loss. 'No, no. I'll come down tomorrow.'

The funeral is a shabby affair. Tom has no family and only Effie, her sister Lizzie and her husband Bill, walk behind the coffin. Her landlady arrives unexpectedly, clothed in heavy black crepe, and is mistaken for Tom's mother by the funeral director. There are no representatives from The Blue Anchor where Tom has spent most of his adult life. Effie would have liked Bridget to have come but is embarrassed by the lack of floral tributes and funeral tea. She watches the thin wooden coffin disappear behind a cheap pink curtain (into the fires of hell, Effie hopes) and leaves the little chapel for a port and lemon at the pub with Lizzie. She notices a young man in a camel coat with a black velvet collar sitting at the back. A 'wide boy' her mother would have called him. They do not speak. No condolences are offered. His cheeks are wet.

Effie is given a week's compassionate leave from work. It is enough. Each morning she does not pin up her hair or bother to dress properly and wears her slippers all day. She gazes out of the back window at the grey washing flapping drearily in the yard and sits smoking and drinking pot after pot of weak tea. For the benefit of the neighbours, she has drawn the curtains in the front room. She is unable to watch the comings and goings in the street outside, but she can eat chips straight from the newspaper at eight o'clock at night without being seen. She listens to band music and comedies on the wireless and even laughs out loud occasionally. On Sunday mornings she does not get out of bed until gone half past eight. She hopes Tom is looking down on her from wherever he is, and fuming.

Effie swishes out her teacup under the tap. She never thought she would be sick of the taste of tea, but she is now. She does not know what 'mourning' should feel like – surely it can't be the confusion she is feeling now?

Effie thinks about the women's gossip at The Bright Hour, the childish giggling at the vicar's wife's expense, the lengthy debates about the quality of cakes on offer that week. She misses the singing, and the opportunity to sit on those cold, hard chairs and think about nothing-in-particular when the prayers begin. She even misses the doubtful pleasures of the weekly Beetle Drive. She recalls the roughness of Bridget's hands, the smell of lavender on her handkerchief, her eyes with a hint of suggestion in them (which she welcomes but doesn't really understand.)

The following week Effie arrives home from work tired and irritable after a slipped bike chain has prolonged her journey. She sees someone waiting at her front door. It is the young man in the camel coat who had been at the back of the chapel at Tom's funeral. His hair lies trapped beneath a slick of hair oil and he has pock-marked skin, red blotches and scars covering both cheeks and forehead. When he speaks his voice is unpleasantly nasal.

'Sorry to bother you love. Remember me? You must've wondered who the hell I was at Tom's funeral. Too upset to introduce myself. Tom was a good pal of mine. A very good pal. I was gutted to hear about the bomb. Terrible business. Jim. Jim's my name. How do?'

'He never mentioned you.' Effie's voice is flat. She is suspicious and a nauseous dread begins to snake from her stomach to her throat. She props up her bike, finds her key and walks towards the front door.

'We did a lot of work together, partners sort of…'

'Work?' Effie turns back. 'Tom never did any work.'

'Oh, he did love. He may not have mentioned it to you. Didn't want to worry you I s'pose.'

'Why would I be worried?' Effie does not want a reply to this question.

'He sort of looked out for men like me, you know, the law and that. A real gent. Course, being a homosexual himself he knew the ropes.'

'A homosexual?' Effie leans on the door jamb to prevent herself falling. Jim opens his eyes wide.

'Sorry love. Thought you knew.' He pauses. 'Anyway, he promised me some money just last week. To help me get back on me feet. He told me to come round here to get it. A hundred pounds.'

'A hundred pounds?' says Effie. 'I haven't got a hundred pounds. Look at me. D'you think I'd be living in a place like this if I had a hundred quid going spare?'

'That's OK sweetheart. I'll come back next week. Tuesday – about this time. If not me, it'll be a couple of me mates. Nothing to worry about. I promise you that if you give me the hundred the law need never know what went on with Tom and…'

He shrugs and laughs as he begins to saunter down the street. Effie stands very still on the doorstep. He looks back over his shoulder.

'See ya Tuesday then.'

Effie goes to The Bright Hour with Bridget the next day. She does not participate much in the general chatter when they arrive at the hall. During the service she tries praying. She thinks that Jesus would indeed have to be a bloody miracle worker to get her out of this one.

On Thursday, Effie and Bridget have a cigarette break in the filthy little alley next to the factory. Bridget stands against the sooty wall with her eyes closed, her face tipped up to catch the weak afternoon sun.

'I was one leg short of a beetle yesterday,' she says. 'We could have been having a fish supper tonight.' She stops and opens her eyes. 'OK. Out with it, Effie. What's up?'

Effie hesitates. She stubs out her cigarette.

'I had a visitor last night,' she says. 'Some bloke. Said he knew Tom. Asked me for a hundred quid.'

'A hundred quid?' says Bridget. 'What the bloody hell for?" She takes a loose cigarette from her pocket and tucks it behind her ear.

'He said Tom promised him it.' Effie feels wretched. 'Said Tom was a homosexual.' She pauses. 'I'm so scared Bridge. He knows where I live and says he's coming round for the money next week.'

Bridget turns Effie to face her, leans forwards and kisses her on the lips. They pull away startled, and stare into each other's faces. How soft Bridget's lips are Effie thinks, and how much more enjoyable that was than the kisses demanded of her by Tom, on his grizzled, beer-stained mouth.

Effie climbs the steps to the police station. She enters through the heavy blue wooden door with its square glass windows. She is wearing her wedding/funeral coat for a bit of Dutch courage. She has done nothing wrong yet what she has to say feels like a confession. A policeman stands behind the counter, his large red face perspiring profusely and his uniform jacket buttoned so tightly that his neck bulges above his shirt collar. He is licking the end of his pencil and frowning with concentration. Effie suspects football pools but he puts his arm down so that she cannot see.

'Morning madam. What can I do for you?'

'I need to talk to someone about a man who is asking me for money.' She wants to get this over with.

'Right.' The policeman lowers his voice and says not unkindly: 'Debt collector, is it?'

'No. Nothing like that. I don't know this man. He says he knew my husband. My husband has recently passed away.'

'Sorry for your loss,' says the policeman. He looks through the window as though the funeral cortege itself is passing at that very moment. But then he winks and leads Effie into a small interview room.

'D'you fancy a cuppa?'

'No, no thank you.'

A younger man in an ill-fitting suit comes into the room. He is distant, preoccupied with something else but introduces himself politely enough as Inspector something-or-other. He sits, relaxes a little and looks closely at her.

'Right. So, what's been going on here?'

Effie tells her story aware he is not listening very closely. He is reading something in the file in front of him and suddenly interrupts her.

'Can you describe this man? What did he look like?'

'Quite young. Fair hair with lots of Brylcreem and -'

'Camel coat. Bad acne. Is this him?' He takes a blurred photo from his file. Effie studies it carefully.

'Yes. That's him. D'you know him?' The inspector smirks.

'Jimmy Stoyles? Oh yes. Good friend of ours. Got a nice little racket going with recently bereaved widows, sorry for your loss incidentally. Goes to the funeral and appears to be very upset, quite the little actor, then visits and tells the widow he knows something,' he pauses, 'unsavoury shall we say, about their husbands. Sound familiar?'

'He said my husband was a homosexual,' says Effie.

'Oh yes, that's one of his lines. Asked you for money?'

'A hundred pounds. He's coming back for it next week. I haven't got it…'

'Course you haven't and even if you did you wouldn't want to be giving it to Jimmy. He's got a record for this sort of thing. Used to have a partner - two of them in it together. Did he mention anyone else?'

Effie is silent. She looks down at the table.

'Look.' The inspector takes a small square card from the file. 'This is me. We'll pay Jimmy a visit today and if you hear another squeak out of him, you just come back and tell us.'

Effie walks slowly down the steps of the police station and looks back at the blue lamp burning above the door. It has started to rain again, and she has forgotten her umbrella.

That evening she searches for Tom's letter. It is still lying in the pocket of her old coat in the wardrobe. She opens it carefully and reads it quickly. It contains the news she had expected. There is someone else in Tom's life although Rose is not mentioned by name. At the end he writes 'with love from Tom' and for some reason this makes her cry for the first time since hearing about his death. She does not believe he ever loved her nor she him, but now she wonders if he had in fact loved someone else all along. Someone who was not necessarily Rose Netherstreet, God rest her soul. She thinks about what Jimmy Stoyles has told her. Is this something Tom has carried with him throughout their entire married life? Surely not but it explains a lot. She remembers the ring which was amongst Tom's personal effects. She had not recognised it. She is sad for him but even sadder for herself. She would like to speak to Jimmy, to throw some light on the man Tom really had been.

Since their first kiss in the alley next to the factory there have been many more. Effie and Bridget are becoming more confident by the day. There has even been some furtive unbuttoning of blouses and dresses. Some encounters have taken place on a piece of wasteland behind the church hall and so for them both, their little talks with Jesus appear to be paying dividends.

They plan a weekend in Brighton. No-one thinks this is strange. Effie has been cruelly widowed and deserves a treat. How kind of Bridget to take her away. Effie buys a new blouse on the never-never – it is cream broderie anglaise with pink ribbon on the collar, just the thing for a fish supper she thinks. She sits at the kitchen table every evening making a list of what she needs to pack. She thinks about her schooldays, her crush on the maths teacher, how she would have done anything, anything, for the captain of the girls' hockey team. Most of the girls had crushes but she had always felt hers went far deeper, that she would have willingly acted upon them given the chance, though quite what that would have looked like she does not know. But she had never been given that chance and her longings remained hidden.

A candle in a milk bottle is on the table when they eat their fish supper in Brighton. They both agree the chips aren't as good as those at home. Their digs are in an old house which needs a new coat of paint, and which is fronted by a dusty yard of dying shrubs. But their room is clean, and they are close to the sea. The landlady is tall and prim with a nose you could hem a skirt with Bridget says. She looks at them knowingly but says nothing. When they stroll along the prom, they see other women arm in arm, and men walking together with shoulders touching, their faces close together as they talk or light cigarettes for each other. Sometimes a flash of recognition passes between them, a slight smile, the raising of an eyebrow. Over a milk stout in The Prince of Wales on the pier, Effie and Bridget talk about staying there forever.

One day in the market, Effie sees Jimmy Stoyles. He has a bruised eye and a large cut across his forehead. He sees her before she sees him and pushes through the crowds, ducking behind fruit and vegetable stalls to get away from her. She finds him later in the Pie and Mash shop and without speaking sits down opposite him. He half stands to go before looking at his pie, the bright green liquor spreading like an oily lake around his plate, and he sits down again. There is a long silence.

'Can't blame me for trying,' he says and almost smiles.

'What happened to your face?' says Effie.

'Some blokes just don't like the cut of me jib,' he says. He grins. Effie orders a cup of tea. They sit in silence again until it arrives.

'I want to know about Tom.' Jimmy's pie continues to congeal on the plate.

'Meant what I said. He was a good pal to me. And he was good at the widow stuff though he hated the old biddies.'

'But the money?' says Effie. 'He must have made a fair bit. What happened to that?' Jimmy swirls pie crust in the green liquor with his fork.

'He had a flat. Deptford, I think. Never went there. Never invited.'

Effie drinks her tea, but Jimmy does not eat.

'What about you?' she says. Jimmy looks up.

'I'm alright,' he says. 'The bastards'll never catch me.' He laughs loudly, but all Effie hears is an anguished howl.

Effie bundles up Tom's clothes in an old suitcase to take to the Salvation Army. She works quickly and carelessly, afraid of what she may find but checking the pockets for loose change. Everything goes except his galoshes which she thinks might come in handy.

Bridget and Effie spend Christmas together. They toast each other in cooking sherry, pull crackers over a chicken dinner, and spend the rest of the day in bed. It is the best Christmas Effie can ever remember. On Boxing Day, they stroll around Southwark Park and Bridget says:

'They'll soon get to know at work y'know Effie. Those bitches on the production line will lap it up.'

'Wish I could say I don't care,' Effie says.

'It'll blow over.'

The mutterings and jibes go on a good deal longer than either Bridget or Effie expect. Some women no longer speak to them. Some push them to the back of the line on Fridays when free bags of broken biscuits are distributed. A knees-up at The Blue, or a Beetle Drive win help steady the ship but the secret which can never be divulged is always there.

They are welcomed back to The Bright Hour. They have been missed. Nothing much has changed. The women view them as one entity now – Bridget-and-Effie. They are aware of others – Esther-and-Grace, Olive-and-Winnie - and they wonder, but nothing is said. The vicar's wife in her Spring hat of cream straw with wilting felt daisies, continues to deliver the message of a church which neither accepts nor understands. The whispered secrets of so many lives drift through the air and up into the rafters, unheard.

The Sandcastle

Joyce arrives at the beach beneath a thunder-blue sky. She had hoped to have the wide expanse of yellow sand to herself for half an hour. But already the crowds are streaming down the concrete ramp, loaded with towels and chairs, chattering, and milling around on the beach. They are invading her space, and she resents every one of them.

She settles near the wooden hut where deckchairs are hired out. She has a good view of the rest of the beach from here. She cannot afford a deckchair herself, and glares at the growing queue of those who can. Surely the children don't need a deckchair to themselves! Are these people made of money? And no doubt there'll be ice creams and chips later, and toys purchased by parents who always give in, who do anything to keep the kids quiet.

Joyce lays a beach mat (an extravagant purchase at the beginning of the season) and her towel carefully on the sand, securing each corner with a small rock. She lowers herself down, her hips and knees creaking painfully. Hot, silver rivulets of sand run between her toes, and over her legs and elbows.

The heatwave has lasted for two weeks. A smoky haze shimmers above the sea, and the horizon beneath the silver-white sky is indistinct. There are no clouds, no breeze and already the atmosphere is heavy and cloying.

Joyce watches as more territory is claimed, mainly by fathers who establish ownership with plastic chairs and cool boxes. The crowd are not all holiday makers. She recognises the woman from the baker's shop with her daughter, a few young girls who ought to be at school, the young man who once came round to mend her washing machine. She does not acknowledge them. She has a strange feeling that none of them have the right to be there. They have other lives to lead. She only has the beach.

Thin cotton sunshades rise precariously from mounds of sand. Red-faced men press the metal poles down as far as they will go. Nearby a green plastic crocodile is tethered to a windbreak with a skipping rope. Squirming toddlers are smothered in lardy cream, impatient to get down to the important business of digging and damming. Behind Joyce a couple are laughing as they grapple with the mechanics of their rented deckchairs. Joyce stares at them.

As soon as the sun comes out people don't care how much flesh they expose, she thinks. Look at him over there. That great big glistening belly hanging over his shorts like brown custard. And her. She'll be falling out of that bikini any minute. Her irritation grows. Where do they think they are? Even to her own ears she sounds prim.

Cigarettes are lit, magazines and puzzle books produced, beer bottles popped open. A football pitch has been drawn in the wet sand with a child's spade. Joyce watches a group of young men attempt to play. After a few kicks the crowd encroach upon their game, and they return to their towels.

Nearby Joyce becomes aware of a woman shoving two cheap metal-framed chairs into drifts of sand. They are covered with faded canvas and likely to split at any minute. Despite their dubious reliability, the father of the family (or could it be an uncle? Too young for a grandad but these days who knows?) sits down heavily and closes his eyes. His wife (girlfriend probably, Joyce sniffs) has already struggled with a buggy not designed to be wheeled across dry sand. Joyce does not offer to help her. The infant inside is hot and grizzly. Joyce's heart sinks. It'll be crying all day, and right next to her. Sandwiches wrapped in foil hang out of a shabby Arsenal rucksack alongside a box of fizzy drinks and crisps. The mother places a rubber flip flop at her feet ready to throw at fearless gulls who swoop perilously close to any edible pickings.

It is hotter than ever. Joyce longs for shade and wishes she had the courage to walk down to the sea. Well, why not? She could just paddle for a while to cool off. But the shallows are crawling with people splashing and yelling, and several children are screaming with excitement. Their voices are piercing and go right through her head. She lays down and tries to doze but the sounds and smells around her are too intrusive. She sits up again.

A second child in the family, a boy of about three, is toddling industriously from sea to beach with his bucket, unperturbed that the water he collects so carefully and tips into the small hole he has dug sinks without trace. He fills his bucket and turns it upside down, tapping it enthusiastically. Untidy piles of sand cascade out. His mother looks over at him.

'Alright Davey?' she says, stretching her arm out towards him. Satisfied he is engaged with the task in hand, she lets her arm drop and turns back to her magazine and immersion in celebrity gossip.

Joyce is appalled. Why aren't they playing with Davey or at least keeping a closer eye on him? Anything could happen. He could wander off, perhaps even go into the sea on his own. He is muttering, quiet infant gibberish, asking himself questions and answering them, sometimes humming as he worked. His sibling has fallen asleep at last. His parents take advantage of this lull and fall asleep themselves.

Joyce remembers days at the beach with her own parents. It was such a treat, a rare occasion when she did not feel a burden to them. Her father made quite a thing of it, insisting everyone enjoy themselves. The beach was not so crowded then. When she had brought them here the year before they died, they were so shocked at the number of people, the litter, the sheer excess of everything, that she wished they had stayed at home.

Joyce had done her duty. She had cared for them as long as she could. But when they went into the nursing home, she watched the funds from the sale of their bungalow slipping away until there was nothing left, and they were at the mercy of the local authority. That had been very hard to bear.

She falls asleep and wakes with a start, aware she has started dribbling on to her towel. She hopes she has not been snoring. It is three o'clock. She stands up stiffly, brushes sand from her legs and feet. She aches all over as she rolls up her beach mat and towel and pulls a dress over her costume, balancing awkwardly on the shifting sandy hillocks. With sandals dangling from one finger, she turns to go.

Davey, who has drawn closer to her during the afternoon, stops his castle building and turns to stare. Under his appraising gaze, Joyce somehow feels she owes him an explanation.

'I'm off for an ice cream,' she says. Her voice is husky after three days of speaking to no-one. She begins to trudge up the beach, unaware that Davey is following her. At the ice cream kiosk, she leans her elbows on the warm sticky counter. Turning her head slightly she notices him standing behind her, finger in mouth and spade in hand.

'D'you want one?' she says. After a pause, he nods glumly.

'Here y'are Sonny Jim.' The ice cream man passes him a cornet which he clutches in small sandy hands.

'That's seven pounds love.'

'Seven pounds! I remember when '99s' cost ninety-nine pence.' The ice cream man does not reply. Joyce and Davey stand together in the shade of the promenade. The ice creams are melting fast. Joyce looks down at him and spits on a tissue to dab around his mouth.

'D'you fancy a ride in my car?'

She has spoken without thinking and does not know where this has come from. Davey hesitates but as she continues up the ramp, she knows he is behind her. They reach the main road. She takes his hand. He is still busy eating his cornet and when they arrive beside her car, he holds his hands up for her to clean them. She carefully wipes between each finger with the corner of her dress. She opens the driver's door, throws her beach paraphernalia on to the back seat, and opens the passenger door for him. Obediently he clambers in beside her. She manoeuvres the car out on to the coast road and looks down at him. He is staring out of the window.

They are long gone before a woman's wail drifts across the bay. They do not see the panicking parents followed by others running around the beach calling out Davey's name, or the ice cream vendor pointing in her direction.

As they drive Joyce is more confident than ever that taking Davey home with her is the right thing to do. He will be happy with her. She will make sure of that.

For years, several times a day, Joyce has passed the charity shop near the bus stop. Sometimes she studies the collections of unwanted milk jugs, old bottles of hand cream, cups without saucers, pairs of showy shoes (worn once and probably pinched, she thinks.) She has never been inside. That would be crossing a line. She could never appear in public wearing someone else's cast-off cardigan. It would be some kind of admission of defeat. But today she pushes open the door clutching Davey's hand, feeling the weight of a twenty-pound note, her 'emergency haul', lying in her purse.

There are two other customers. One is a London blow-in wearing expensive trainers and showy glasses, peering beneath pieces of pottery for a valuable find. The other, a woman wearing a blouse the colour of porridge, is pulling cotton dresses from the rails, checking the size, and putting them back again. A third woman with sparkling eye shadow and an important bottom, bustles over towards them.

'Can I help?' she says. Her smile exposes a thick band of pink gum and tiny teeth.

'No thank you,' says Joyce. 'We're just looking.'

'Looks like your grandson has looked and has found,' says the woman grinning at Davey. They watch him head for a large yellow tractor and sit down on the floor to play with it. Joyce feels the woman is far too familiar and moves away from her although she has felt a thrill at the word 'grandson.'

The shop does not have the smell she expected – dirty underwear and old women's lavender water. It is well organised. She can see the children's clothes neatly lined up on a rack near the door at the back. Davey is now driving the tractor through a zoo where animals in tiny enclosures have been set out on a low table. He is delighted as various species of African wildlife fly into the air, and the woman rushes forward to pretend that part of Davey's game involves putting the animals back again. He is humming to himself, and then starts to talk but too quietly for Joyce to hear what he is saying. He has not spoken much at all. She longs to have some kind of conversation with him. It will come she assures herself. Just a matter of time.

Joyce finds a waterproof jacket she thinks might fit him, a couple of reasonably clean tee shirts, and some green corduroy trousers. He is still wearing the filthy tee shirt he was wearing yesterday which he refused to remove when she tucked him in to her bed last night. He is also still wearing his shorts and she is aware of a vague aroma of urine. She wonders if she can risk pulling the trousers over them there in the shop. There is no children's underwear for sale and so she thinks the trousers and the shorts will have to do for the moment. She looks round and sees Davey has found a red cotton baseball cap with 'Grandad's Little Helper' emblazoned across the front. He has pulled it right down over his eyes. She is about to rush forward to remove it and then thinks that perhaps in this weather and under these circumstances it wouldn't be a bad buy.

Davey refuses to remove the cap when they leave the shop and won't give up the tractor she has bought against her better judgement. Plastic junk, she thinks but he was clutching it too tightly for her to pull it away without making a scene. They begin to walk home. She is looking forward to spending more time with him on her own. It had not been easy last night. She thinks this will pass. Eventually.

She glances down at the ping of her local Newsfeed. She stops suddenly. She places her hands on Davey's shoulders as she reads the message which has appeared on the screen.

> "HAVE YOU SEEN THIS BOY?
> Davey is 3 years old with blonde curly hair and blue eyes.
> He was last seen on the Town Beach some time yesterday afternoon.
> He was wearing red swimming shorts and a Spiderman tee shirt.
> Anyone with any information please call the police on this number."

Joyce stands rigid with shock. Her hands are pressing down hard on Davey's shoulders now, and he is trying to release himself from her grip. They don't even know what time he went missing, she thinks.

Joyce drags Davey along the street as fast as she dares. As they reach the house her neighbours Ken and Lesley are arriving on their motorbike. The message has thrown her, and she almost pushes Davey inside without acknowledging their greeting. She can feel their eyes on her back. She knows that Lesley will be dying to know who Davey is. Well, let her guess, thinks Joyce. I don't care. Us two are happy and that's all that counts. She opens the back door and Davey goes outside to play with his tractor although she feels uneasy about this.

Later, they sit in the front room after a disappointing lunch. The sausage and beans had not been a great success last night and although he has nibbled on the beefburger today, he has not touched the vegetables. She knows that what he really wants is chips. He had looked up at her hopefully outside the fish and chip shop near the park, but she did not give in. They are bad for him – greasy and full of God knows what. They were probably his staple diet before she rescued him. Now she will introduce him to food which is good for him – hot, nourishing, green, and freshly cooked.

Davey lies listlessly on the floor, bored with his tractor. He starts to grizzle. A knock at the door silences him. He looks up at Joyce as she makes her way warily to the window. The curtains are thin enough for her to see two figures outside and she ducks back before they see her. They knock again, more urgently. Joyce carefully lifts Davey off the floor and gently pulls his baseball cap down over his curls. Such pretty curls, she thinks. But distinctive. If only she had trimmed them off last night as she had planned. If only they had gone off this morning to the caravan park a few miles inland. If only she had tried harder to keep Davey quiet during the night. The nightmare, the screaming. That will have done it. Ken and Lesley will have heard it, seen the message, and put two and two together. They would have been on to the police as quick as you like. She was not surprised. She had never liked them, with their water feature and their illuminated bunting and their gas barbecue, and those ridiculous glasses of pina colada they drank in the back yard. Oh, she'd seen them from her bedroom window alright. They will love the drama of all this. Probably hope to be interviewed by local TV tonight.

She picks up her bag from the table, and her swimming costume from the back of the chair, and Davey's spade standing by the back door. Lifting the latch quietly she smiles down at him and takes his hand. She leads him across the parched yellow grass to the car parked behind the house. They get in – there is no hurry, no panic. She feels quite calm. As she fixes his seatbelt, the letterbox is opened, and she hears someone calling her name. The car engine starts. There is a shout as she drives down the back alley and on to the main road. Davey looks up at her with an expression of mild alarm but is soon distracted by a broken pen and a dusty Opal Fruit he has found on the seat.

Joyce drives to another bay further along the coast. She parks in the small carpark behind the beach. They make their way to the sands down some unstable metal steps (an accident waiting to happen, she thinks.) There is no queue for deckchairs here. The attendant is lounging on a sunbed playing with his mobile. She decides both she and Davey deserve a treat. She raps on the hut to get the attendant's attention glaring accusingly at his tattoos and drags a deckchair on to a patch of gravelly shingle well away from the crowds. She lifts Davey up, but he is not interested in the deckchair and within seconds he has slid off. He busies himself building an untidy extension to a large sandcastle abandoned by another child earlier in the day. A paper flag protrudes from one side. Davey uses the wooden stick to make patterns in the sand. Joyce makes a half-hearted attempt to join in with the game, but he makes it clear he prefers to work alone.

She shades her eyes with her hands. The sun is not so strong today and some wispy white-grey clouds have appeared on the horizon. Keeping a close eye on Davey, she changes into her costume and walks down to the sea. She removes her sandals, placing them neatly together on the sand where it meets the incoming tide. She paddles across the shallow water avoiding the razor fish shells but sliding on greasy clumps of waving seaweed. She wades into deeper water, sometimes stopping as the waves break around her body. The water is very cold. She feels numb as she plunges ahead. Eventually she is out of her depth.

The water raises her up and she starts to swim but she is exhausted and can barely tread water as she turns to face the beach. She thinks she can just about spot Davey still playing with his spade by the deckchair but when she looks again, she thinks maybe it is not him at all. Suddenly she is afraid. Her legs feel weak as she kicks against the current to reach shallower water. She wades back to the shore.

An early exodus from the beach has started as the rain, at last, begins to fall. She finds herself running towards the deckchair but can already see that Davey is not there. Grabbing her dress and her bag she looks around the emptying beach. The sandcastle has been trampled upon and Davey's cap lies partially buried in its ruins. She picks it up and finds she is sobbing. This is ridiculous she tells herself, but the sobs are coming thick and fast. She stumbles blindly down towards the sea.

And then she sees him. He is crouching near a channel of water, damming the flow with stones and seaweed. He is totally engrossed and does not notice her approach. Next to him a woman is gathering towels and fussing two children into kagoules. She glances over at Davey. Joyce swallows hard.

'There you are,' she says. She pulls the cap down on his head, holds out her hand to him, and says more loudly than she intended. 'Come on Robert. Time to go.'

Seaview Cosy Guesthouse fails on all counts. An oily-curtained no-questions-asked establishment, Joyce and Davey stay there for two weeks. It is grim but Joyce has plans. She spends much of the first week hunched in her car trying to keep Davey amused, waiting for Ken and Lesley to leave on their motor bike. Then she hurries into her house and fills two shabby suitcases with as many things as possible before scuttling out again. She tries to make it a game and tells Davey she is a clever burglar but then realises this is too near the truth. She contacts the landlord and cancels her tenancy. She abandons her car in a large Aldi car park. She feels released.

It has been over a year now since they moved into this cheerless wooden cabin, little more than a shack, on the edge of Romney Marsh. It is bleak but cheap, private, and fifty miles from the coast. Davey has found the transition difficult. He cried and screamed most nights for the first week or two calling for mam and someone called Mikey. In desperation, Joyce took him to a small copse behind the cabin where he began to dig with his spade. She helped him make a den out of some fallen branches and eventually all he wanted to do was to go and play there – alone.

Joyce has established a 'you-must-only-play-where-I-can see-you' zone for Davey. He does not respond well to such a restriction, and she spends much of her time going to find him and hauling him back so that he is always in her sight. Apart from catching the irregular bus to the village for provisions they see few people.

It is a strange time for them both. Often Davey, never a great conversationalist, does not speak at all. He collects stones and feathers and arranges them in patterns on the floor of the cabin. He mumbles to himself and often becomes genuinely distressed for no apparent reason. Then he will start fighting her, little fists punching the air as she tries to calm him.

One day just before Christmas, they have a visitor. Joyce opens the door to a small woman sporting a downy moustache and wearing a shapeless grey felt hat. She twitches nervously, discouraged by Joyce's lack of welcome.

'Hallo there,' she says with creditable bravado. 'I'm Mrs Gleddon, the vicar's wife.'

'Yes?' says Joyce.

'I'm from St Martin's. I was just passing and thought I'd drop in to invite you to the Christmas service.' (Just passing? thinks Joyce. My eye!)

'No thank you,' says Joyce. 'I'm not a believer.'

'Oh,' says Mrs Gleddon. 'And what about the little boy? We have Sunday School every week. You would both be very welcome.' Joyce thinks there is a threatening glint in her eye.

'No. Thank you. Good morning.' Joyce closes the door as gently as good manners allow. Her fear manifests itself in anger. How dare this woman arrive unannounced and try to insinuate herself into their home? She returns to the living room where Davey is battling with a jigsaw. Joyce could never be accused of not trying. She has long conversations with Davey but there is rarely a response. It slowly dawns on her that perhaps Davey has become her imaginary childhood friend and, although the relationship is now a motherly one, she begins to act out the games she remembers from that time. She pretends they are cowboys on the prairie and makes a small fire outside where they cook sausages on the end of long sticks, and she sings 'Home on The Range.' As Robin Hood, she chases him through the wood. She builds him a castle out of some felled boughs intertwined with twigs, with rough leafy turrets fashioned from gorse bushes. Then she is a giant prowling around outside while he is inside screaming with delighted fear. On these occasions she thinks she has never been happier. She believes that Davey is warming towards her. He comes to her for comfort after spotting dog walkers who frighten him. He begins to ask her questions although he doesn't always listen to her replies. Gradually he no longer mentions mam or Mikey although the nightmares continue for many months.

After a while reports about his disappearance dry up and Joyce is glad. She cannot imagine life without him now. Perhaps it will all blow over she thinks. People will forget, they always do. They can never be relied upon, and soon she will be able to keep Davey without that ever-present anxiety.

Joyce is standing at the window one morning staring aimlessly at the fog blanketing the trees. There is a loud rap on the door. Mrs Gleddon, trembling with distress, her top lip damp with perspiration, cries out:

'You'd better come. There's been an accident…'

Joyce leaps out of the door and runs with thumping heart towards the wood. She can see Davey's castle has fallen sideways and when she arrives, he is lying beneath it, his leg pinned to the ground by two of the boughs, a third across his chest. 'This is my fault,' she says under her breath. 'I did this.'

'Call an ambulance.' She shouts at Mrs Gleddon who is already jumping around in the field waving her mobile in the air for a signal. Joyce kneels beside Davey and takes his hand. His face is paper-white, and he is not conscious. She has no idea what to do. She croons and strokes his arm until, after what feels like a hundred years, help arrives.

Joyce sits beside Davey in the ambulance hearing nothing of the ambulance woman droning on about something or other. She provides her name and says he is Robert, providing a fictitious date of birth for him. At the hospital she trots alongside his trolley trying to take his hand. At the end of the corridor, she is instructed to leave him and wait. She hesitates but he is already being wheeled through some swing doors and she has not been invited to go with him.

Joyce sits down in a brightly lit waiting room. It is familiar. She remembers sitting here on so many occasions, waiting to be told whether one or other of her parents had survived their latest health crisis. She recalls how, with an all-consuming guilt, she prays that this time they hadn't. She looks at the posters on the wall instructing her to check for signs of cancer and other life-terminating illnesses. Her worry about Davey escalates and she finds she is having trouble breathing.

At last, the door opens. A nurse comes in and calls her name. Joyce follows her to an open door in the corridor and the nurse ushers her inside. Sitting behind a desk the doctor is not forthcoming and she hovers around opposite him. He looks up and gives her a vague smile.

Does he even know who I am? she thinks irritably. After a great deal of fiddling around with a fountain pen and some charts on his desk, he opens a packet of mints (he does not offer Joyce one) and begins to speak.

'The operation has gone very well. We have saved the leg, but the lung has been slightly punctured, and Robert has lost a lot of blood. However, the prognosis is good. He's comfortable now. His unusual blood group could have been problematic but fortunately we had enough blood in the bank. He will need more, and we will need to replenish our stocks.' He smiles slightly. 'The good news is that we have contacted the handful of people in the county with the same blood group and I'm sure one of them will come forward to help.' He begins writing in his notes and does not look at her.

'Now, I need some information about Robert. Do you have the name and address of his GP?'

'No, I don't.' Joyce sits very still. He looks at her over his half-moon spectacles.

'Right.' He looks down again. Joyce pauses. Without thinking too much she says: 'He's Ukrainian.' The doctor looks up now.

'Ukrainian?'

'Yes, he's only been here two months. His parents are still in Kherson.' Her eyes fill with tears. She really is rather good at this.

'That must be very painful for you. I'm so sorry. How did Robert get here?'

'Neighbours from his village brought him. I collected him from Dover.'

Oh no, not Dover she screams inside her head. That's where the boat people arrive not the Ukrainians. She ploughs on.

'The neighbours have family there.' Not very convincing but it would have to do. She has the doctor's full attention.

'As his grandmother, I expect all the paperwork came to you?'

'Yes,' she says faintly. He pats her hand in a way she does not like.

'Look, don't worry. Just bring everything you have the next time you come. The important thing is that we get Robert well again.'

Joyce stands to go, picks up her bag and her coat. He follows her to the door and opens it. When they are outside, he says:

'I'd leave Robert now. He's sleeping but pop back tonight.' She does not reply. The same nurse approaches and speaks in a low voice to the doctor. He looks up and smiles at Joyce who is already sidling towards the exit.

'Ah,' he says. 'This is good. One of our donors is here already.' Joyce turns and looks down the corridor. In scuffed red Doc Marten boots, Davey's mother is hurrying towards them.

Restored

Alison received her first obscene phone call when she was in her mid-fifties. It was a Friday evening; she felt lazy and was putting off preparations for bed for as long as possible. A man with an unpleasant husky drawl and a strong Birmingham accent said:

'You've got a lovely voice.'

'Have I?' she said.

'Yes. The voice of someone who wears black, lacy knickers. Am I right?'

She hesitated and replied not quite truthfully. She was enough of a woman of the world to know that silk thongs were infinitely more enticing than her extra-large high-waisted support pants.

'Do you like the feel of silk against your body?' he said.

'It's quite nice,' she said although she could not recall ever experiencing it.

'Just listening to you makes me feel quite horny. Do you know what I'm doing now?'

She could hazard a guess. His breath became heavier, and he begged her to keep talking. She was not sure what to say but found continuing with the subject of underwear appeared to work. It was unsophisticated, uncomplicated drivel but as the call progressed, she found she had quite a knack for it.

'You naughty girl. That was amazing.' Her description of some recently purchased rambling socks was abruptly cut off. She was taken off guard by his compliment and agreed that he could contact her again. She was neither shocked nor appalled but afterwards felt quite unsettled and way out of her comfort zone.

Alison's job involved restoring pieces of classical sculpture mainly at the British Museum but sometimes further afield. The work was intricate and often intense, teasing and stroking, carving and moulding stone and wood. She had always found these to be very intimate activities. Thinking about it later, and she did begin to think about it quite often, she thought she might be able to use her work in some way should her caller ever contact her again.

Alison travelled to London every day, resigned to standing for forty minutes on filthy trains which were always crowded and usually late. Jammed on the tube she was offended by the proximity of other people - their smells, the feel of their coats against her legs, their yawns, their loud guffaws. When she walked from Holborn to the museum through damp grey streets, confronted by petrol fumes and noise, she wondered if the despised daily commute was worth it. But when she arrived at the vast empty space on the lower ground floor of the museum, ready to start work, her spirits lifted a little. These were the kind of people with whom she felt comfortable – cold, silent, and motionless.

She was a short woman, almost entirely spherical, her round head balanced between round shoulders. Her face was pale, her features ill-defined as if they were caving in on themselves and becoming less distinct as she grew older. She did not wear stylishly spattered dungarees or tie her hair back with bright printed cloth like her young colleague Sandy, but favoured woollen skirts worn below the knee, slightly too tight, and matted jumpers the colour of cold porridge. Leather shoes in winter and flat sandals in summer had been ruined by years of varnish, adhesive and particles of clay landing on them, which were now impossible to remove.

Alison's appearance might suggest that there had been few if any romantic encounters in her life. Her thick chestnut hair had thinned, and she wore it pulled tightly back from her face, twisted into a sad little bun at the nape of her neck. Her eyebrows on the other hand had continued to grow. They were thick and bushy and hung over her eyes in a permanent frown giving the impression that this was a woman best left alone.

Alison was capable of delicate artistry, re-modelling fingers and toes, hands and feet, whole torsos, with smooth clay, entwining stone strands of hair around blind-eyed faces, re-aligning limbs damaged by age, carelessness, or neglect. Re-creating such things of beauty gave her the greatest of pleasure – an almost physical thrill. This was fortunate. There were few other thrills in her life.

Alison was still thinking about the phone call the following day as she stood back from her work. Three badly cracked marble figures – a man, a woman and a child clutching a lamb – were now perfect and ready to be exhibited. She washed her hands in the small washbasin in an alcove where tools and clay were stored, and then returned to admire the improvements she had made. She felt proud of what she had achieved. She wished there could be a plaque attributing the restoration of the figures to her – something quite small would have been adequate. Then maybe someone, anyone, might see it, and value what she had done.

Despite her skill and experience, Alison was still a junior assistant at the museum alongside Sandy twenty-five years her junior. Alison knew her face did not fit into some vague management vision for the future which had never been shared in any detail with the craftswomen and men who worked at the museum. It seemed that however hard she worked, however much extra research she did in the vast museum library, taking photographs and making notes to make her work as accurate as possible, she did not get the recognition she believed she deserved. She resented the fact that she would never front a television documentary like an ex-colleague of hers, whose grey hair was now dyed an unlikely shade of red, and whose sagging lips pouted inappropriately in front of Jacobean mansions or crumbling Italian follies. Alison was infuriated when the woman made wild claims about ancient ruins and scant remains which could not possibly be corroborated.

She was drinking a cup of tea later that day while the complicated procedure of statue removal began. From nowhere it seemed, thoughts of Alexander suddenly filled her head and once again it occurred to her that her work and her life all revolved around the past. It had been thirty years since she last saw him, but the memories had not faded much. He was such a bastard, she thought and smiled fondly.

Alison had attended a public lecture at the museum one evening and had immediately felt a strong connection with the distinguished speaker. At the end, she had introduced herself and after some banal small talk about the recent restoration of a building nearby, he said:

'D'you fancy a drink? I know a nice little place in Bloomsbury.' He raised an eyebrow, and she was besotted at once, convincing herself that it was his intellect she was attracted to rather than anything else. At the pub she remembered behaving like a teenager, giggling at everything he said, or gazing up at him as he described what amounted to a precis of his recent book. He began to take shameless advantage of her crush on him.

'You're so sweet Alison. So young. Still optimistic. And that voice! Men must be falling at your feet.' Nothing could have been further from the truth, but Alison leaned forward so that her thick, jaw-length hair covered her face. He told her he was engaged to be married but she did not believe him. A short, passionate affair inevitably followed.

'My fiancé's so clever and beautiful,' he once told her. 'A good combination, eh? I really don't deserve her. She is – exquisite.' He moved his fingers slowly through the air to demonstrate her perfection. Alison disliked the affectation but forgave him everything. It wasn't until she saw the photo in the newspaper that she realised he had been telling the truth all along.

The Friday night phone call provided Alison with a new area for research. She did not like to be ill-prepared for anything and knew that this was something she had to work on. The first porn channels she discovered were mildly shocking, but few actual words were exchanged between the actors. Then she discovered some films produced in the 1970s where various workmen with bodies lathered in baby oil arrived at houses belonging to scantily dressed women, who immediately forgot that the fridge was broken, or that the boiler needed to be repaired. Alison found these films crass and tedious at best and often hilarious. But she listened to the brief dialogue between the main characters and jotted down phrases in her notebook. At work, fashioning smooth limbs on to a marble fabric robe or attaching stone sandals to a rocky plinth, she often talked to herself. It occurred to her that these words of personal encouragement were not so very far away from the phrases she was learning now, to help her tease, coax, and excite a faceless voice on the end of the phone. She read out loud the notes she had made after watching the films and they sounded ridiculous. But when Dan (almost certainly not his real name) eventually called again she was able to practice on him and he was delighted. His reaction was swift and more dramatic than before. Afterwards he praised her effusively.

'God Alison, you're so good at this. Look, I wonder if you could do something for me.' There was a long pause. 'My friend's having a bad time. Wife's left him, she's a bitch, not his fault, and he's really pissed off. He's a nice bloke and I wondered if you'd well, if you'd mind helping him out like you help me? I'd be very grateful, we both would.' Alison did not mind at all. In truth, she rather relished a new male voice to compliment her efforts. And it would make all that research more worthwhile.

It was the beginning of many calls from Dan's friends all of whom seemed to be going through a bad time. She gained in confidence and occasionally punctuated her responses with a throaty groan at a point she hoped was appropriate. She never felt as involved as the men with what was going on; it was usually her voice and not her words which were required. Occasionally, this could get boring. She wrote shopping lists, made notes, and once, whilst listening to heavy breathing and moaning at the other end of the line, she almost completed the Evening Standard crossword. But she was not a stupid woman. She knew exactly what was going on here but the enthusiasm of her callers for what she had to offer was intoxicating and she could not stop.

For several months, Alison had been repairing a badly damaged frieze for a new exhibition. It involved the painstaking removal of many layers of grime and paint and was exacting work. The curator of the exhibition, the woman Alison would like to have been, followed her work with interest.

'Just look at what your work has exposed,' she said. 'A rare beauty. You've brought out the detail and texture of every limb, every fold, every rock in the front here.' She breathed heavily close to Alison's ear. 'Outstanding work!'

Alison felt a wave of excitement wash over her. Anything like this was sadly lacking during her evening phone calls. Any woman would do then. But here it was her expertise and hers alone, which had thrilled the curator and confirmed that her work really did have both intrinsic and extrinsic value.

'Did you see the finished frieze?' she said to Sandy who was scrubbing her hands at the sink. 'It was a bugger to do but I can't believe how it's turned out. How beautiful it is underneath. I feel so – satisfied with it. Looking forward to making a start on the next one.'

Sandy was surprised. It was unlike Alison to say much at all let alone brag. They did not often have the opportunity to talk to each other and Alison would have liked to have talked more. But just then some academics arrived to study the sculptures which were being prepared for the exhibition. At the head of the group, their leader swaggered into the basement area with familiar arrogance. Alison breathed in sharply.

Alexander had not changed much despite significant hair loss and a generous paunch. He won't like that thought Alison. The timbre of his voice was lower and less self-assured, but it still cut across all other voices and filled the room. She recalled it only too well. He turned and looked straight through her before moving away. Alison stood very still.

'Who's that?' she said to Sandy.

'A group of Yanks,' said Sandy. 'Visiting the London Institute. They were here yesterday as well – didn't you see them? One of them's a bit handy. Couldn't take his eyes off my bum.' She carried on cleaning her hands and Alison thought it best not to question her too closely about which one that had been. Hardly aware of what she was doing, she went to the staff room to check the number of the London Institute, and immediately called their switchboard. Yes, Alexander lectured there, and they willingly gave her his number with no questions asked. It had been that easy.

Alison went home early feigning a migraine, and by the time she arrived, she really could feel the first arrows of pain shooting out to a small area just above her left eye. She sat on her bed for a full five minutes before, with shaking fingers, she called Alexander's number. The phone rang out for some time before he answered. His voice was gruff, and he was obviously irritated about being disturbed. She almost hung up but lowering her voice she spoke softly.

'You don't know me, but I must say you have a remarkably sexy voice. I can just imagine you sitting there listening to me.' She stopped and almost gave up again. Come on Alison, you can do this, she told herself. She took a deep breath which she managed to convert to a small moan, not a very sexy one but nevertheless the intention was clear.

'I feel so hot. Do you know what I'm doing right at this moment?'

He paused.

'I don't actually. Why don't you tell me?'

Got you, thought Alison. And after that, it was not difficult to repeat the words she had been asked to say, to describe the things she had been asked to do (but never had) during the countless obscene calls she had received over the past few months. She added her much admired moaning for good measure and some newly invented yelps of pleasure. She heard him pant slightly and worried he might be having a heart attack – he was not as young as he used to be. Finally, she said in a slow, breathy voice: 'Oh Alexander!'

Hearing his name, the effect was immediate. He snapped out of whatever trance he had been in and shouted:

'Who are you? You fucking little whore. Are you recording this? What do you want? Oh Christ!' He was near to tears. Alison felt a tortuous pleasure listening to him and longed to identify herself. But unlike real torture this stopped almost at once. She began to tremble as she switched off her mobile and put it down carefully on the bed. She opened a drawer and pushed it right to the back amongst her underwear. The irony of this did not elude her.

She laid down on the bed and thought about what she had just done, the words she had just been using. She had enjoyed instigating the call, taking control for once, but the whole thing had sounded so - 'depraved' was the only word for it. Her face flushed and she wondered what on earth was happening to her.

Every day she was surrounded by works of art which were both beautiful and lasting. Her entire working life had always brought its own rewards. More than ever before, she appreciated how much this meant to her, and how far away it was from the grubby little phone calls which had brought her nothing at all. Why had it taken her so long to realise this? She felt neither shame nor embarrassment, just a rush of fury and a sense of acute isolation. She wondered now whether accepting the phone calls had had anything to do with a sub-conscious desire to confront Alexander, and to punish him. If so, it had brought her no satisfaction whatsoever and she knew the calls must now stop. She supposed she had Alexander to thank for her road-to-Damascus moment. She had little else to thank him for.

Alison slept well that night and woke early. It was a dull, sultry day, the sun appearing like a glassy yellow mirror behind thin clouds. For the first time in months, she combed her hair and allowed it to hang around her face in thin grey strands. She enjoyed the lack of constriction around the back of her neck and across her hairline. She was looking forward to the day's work. She was starting a new project which would provide a sharp focus; it would be good to talk to Sandy about it. Had it not been for her arthritic knee, she may even have managed a spring in her step. The deep loneliness she had grown to live with had returned of course. But that was the point. She had grown to live with it and somehow that brought its own comfort.

The Leftovers

On December 22nd Anne's descent from vague anxiety to full-blown panic sets in. The harmless but habitual madnesses she blames on ageing and a solitary lifestyle, are magnified.

Rarely able to sleep until she has calculated the percentage of her bedtime novel yet to be read, she now experiences acute insomnia. Identifying prime numbers from any arbitrary list she encounters becomes obsessive. Counting every step she takes up and down staircases is now compulsive. There are more of these quirks, many more. Oh God. Never riddles or rhymes, always numbers, fractions, percentages, perimeters, whizzing around her skull. They would be her undoing. She has no doubt of that.

As the Christmas pantechnicon rolls determinedly towards her and Anne takes on the mantle of planning family celebrations again, the opportunities for calculation multiply. Her mother with whom she lives, is becoming more and more frail so that now, it is Anne who prepares vast quantities of Christmas food, and who provides cursory decorations which, although she does not intend it, appear to be more grudging every year.

Anne is also responsible for purchasing presents for her nephew and niece. These must be parent-approved vouchers of some kind which will be greeted with the obligatory polite thank you and barely disguised disdain. She was tempted to buy her nephew a large yellow tractor driven by an illuminated dinosaur this year, and for her niece, a brightly coloured game involving the construction of a trap to catch the final unlucky player resulting, according to the picture on the front of the box, in much hilarity. She stopped herself. She knows there would be mutterings of 'plastic tat' behind the parents' closed doors on Christmas night.

Anne draws blood on her hands and arms as she cuts down branches of shiny holly and strands of veined ivy in the garden. No berries again this year she thinks as she arranges the foliage along the mantlepiece with as much flair as she can muster. She has bought a small tree from the greengrocer at the end of the road and carried it home with difficulty before balancing it in the old flowerpot kept in the garden shed for this one specific purpose. She removes the dusty box of baubles from the top of the wardrobe and settles her mother in her chair in front of the tree so that she can hang the tin robins and tiny wooden sleighs on the lower branches. After her mother has gone to bed, she feels compelled, as she does every year, to rearrange them so that they form a perfectly symmetrical triangle of hanging decorations. At the end she is left with one grubby angel which does not fit into the pattern. Without much thought, she crumples the tiny wings in her hand and throws the angel into the kitchen bin. She stretches a mean string of tiny lights around the tree. Somehow it looks more shabby and less festive than it did last year. She is not averse to buying new decorations; she knows she ought to but just doesn't have the heart for it.

Her two brothers and their families arrive on Christmas morning. Noise, parcels, glazed food beneath foil lids, crates of wine, screaming excited laughter and discarded shoes fill the house. Anne does not mind this. She is fond of her family and welcomes the activity, if from a distance. She knows the jollity will not last.

Accompanying her mother to church is another of her annual burdens. She thinks of a 'burden' as a solid living thing, a dark brown and heavy spikey creature floating around the house for the entire Christmas period. This and other tasks fall to Anne, or fall on her, unwanted seasonal weights.

Anne knows church will be even worse this year. The words 'awe,' 'wonder' and 'subtle' are not within the new vicar's lexicon. She is an evangelical enthusiast who must have promised to 'shake things up' at the church during her interview. Do vicars have interviews? Anne does not know. What she does know is that this Christmas morning service will be unlike any other her mother has attended.

Anne has not been to church for over a year. Last year she went to a carol service at the Minster where, within an incense-infused atmosphere, she sang carols and became emotional as children lit candles and, in tea-towelled head-dresses, acted out the story of the nativity. Anne knows she has 'lapsed'; she has sunk below the surface of that celestial lake to the dark depths below and God is glaring down on her from above. Anne's mother consistently, and inaccurately, claims to be a committed churchgoer and blames her poor attendance on limited movement and failing eyesight.

The village church is a pretty 17th century grey stone building with decorative turrets and a slim unadorned spire. They arrive early, Anne's mother hanging on to her arm, her arthritic hips causing a drunken sway and a lack of balance. They are welcomed effusively by a woman who has been hovering by the door watching their progress. She is dressed in a sparkly woollen jumper of swirling snowflakes on matted wool. As they shuffle to a pew near the back, Anne realises the woman's outfit is not out of place. Most people are similarly attired, and Anne regrets her pearls and good coat. The vicar is wearing a red shiny headband on top of which sits a small, smug Santa with a flashing hat. Her flowery blouse has a clerical collar neatly integrated into the neckline, an ideal garment in which to flounce around between the pews which she is doing now. Anne, feeling less than charitable, wonders grimly if the woman has become a vicar purely to wear such a thing.

She sits down next to her mother and counts how many people are in attendance. It is a poor turnout – certainly less than last year. She works out that as a percentage of the number of inhabitants in the village, the number is low. But this does not deter the enthusiastic cries of 'Praise the Lord' and the loud whoops of excitement at unexpected moments during the service. Her mother looks around with mild surprise.

The congregation stand, squinting at a crooked screen erected to one side of the pulpit. They sing the first verse of 'It Came Upon a Midnight Clear' three times before the vicar, giggling coyly, announces:

'Technical glitch. As a mere woman I'm afraid I haven't a clue how to put it right. But I know a man who does.'

It is not only the 'mere woman' that rankles so much. Anne glares as the vicar's husband, an over-large Santa hat falling over his eyes, rises and joins the grinning pianist at the side of the church. They fiddle around with a laptop for far too long. Anne's mother shifts uneasily, looking at Anne with raised disapproving eyebrows. She is unsure how such a thing could be happening in church – and on Christmas Day!

The vicar is searching for inspiration divine or otherwise. The congregation begin to murmur amongst themselves. Hymnbooks are distributed hurriedly, thrown along each pew, and Anne's mother grabs one with relief. At last, here is something she recognises and understands. But just then verse two of the Carol appears on the screen and, hymnbooks forgotten, the congregation begin to sing again.

The beautiful old church fidgets with embarrassment. Anne wonders if the service will ever end. Members of the congregation are invited to bring a present they have received to the front of the church, a nightmarish Christmas Show and Tell. A large woman in a red dress cries out 'I'll give you a twirl' as she dances down the aisle. She is followed by a teenager in purple velvet trousers who smiles sheepishly at Anne. The local Councillor, a caricature of himself - plump, perspiring, and self-important - stands to face the congregation and informs them with an unbecoming leer that he is wearing his Christmas pants. There is a sharp intake of breath from Anne's mother.

Anne's mother watches aghast as children rush to the end of the pews to pull crackers with each other across the aisle. The vicar provides a bizarre explanation for this, that in some kind of vague terrible way, it symbolises love between the nations of the world. Paper hats, hackneyed jokes and plastic charms are catapulted from the cardboard missives and land on the beautiful, tiled floor. Anne and her mother stare down at them. They can think of nothing to say to each other. Anne wonders if they might be able to slip away quietly without being noticed. They do not belong here.

Gold-wrapped chocolate coins are being distributed by a group of giggling Girl Guides, and the vicar invites everyone to go and give their coin to someone else with their own personal Christmas message.

'I've got a personal Christmas message for the vicar, haven't you?' whispers Anne to her mother who nods in disbelief. People are standing up now. They leave their seats to go and hug their neighbours, kissing them on the cheek with a little too much enthusiasm.

'Don't move. Just keep looking at me. Don't look right or left…' Anne whispers as she takes her mother's hand.

But it is too late. A thin woman in an electric wheelchair wearing reindeer antlers is wending her way towards them with outstretched arms.

Anne and her mother know that staying to take communion is out of the question. Perhaps the bread and wine will have been replaced by stollen bites and festive punch? Anne would not have been surprised. Her mother takes her arm as they begin their unsteady stagger home. Anne remarks upon the chocolate coin still clutched tightly in the palm of her mother's leather glove. Her mother stops and looks at her, eyes bright within the soft folds of her face.

'No reverence, Anne,' she says. 'Not a shred of reverence or respect. I was blowed if I wasn't going to salvage something from that bloody ridiculous pantomime.'

Anne's mother rarely swears but her fury allows the word to sit comfortably upon her lips. Anne smiles. Her mother does not smile back.

'Do you think events have passed us by?' Anne says. 'Are all church services like this now? Have we simply been left behind.'

'No.' Her mother is angry and visibly upset. 'You don't get those shenanigans on Songs of Praise or the Morning Service. Can you imagine Aled Jones pulling crackers or talking about his pants on national television?'

Anne does not reply. She is also upset but less about the service itself than the feeling that she is travelling on the wrong road. Once again, she has not fitted in.

Anne would have liked to have described the fiasco to the rest of the family but when they return, the familiar chaos has settled itself like a familiar blanket over the lounge and she knows no-one will be listening. She looks at the adults who are drinking pink gins, perched on the sofas, periodically glancing at their mobiles. They have forgotten to turn off the oven as instructed before Anne left for church, and the smell of cooked turkey pervades the whole house. Anne goes into the kitchen to remove it, slightly overdone, from the oven. She returns with bowls of mixed nuts and olives and places them on the small tables scattered around the room. The children are studying their presents, totting up their value to ensure that identical amounts of money have been spent on each of them. Anne is quite interested in this activity and begins to count with them before her older brother Duncan glares at her and shakes his head. Anne's mother sits watching them in silence, a small uncomprehending smile frozen on her lips. Anne does not know how much she enjoys or even understands all this, but her 'family' provides vital material for the stories she will be telling her friends next month at the WI.

Lunch proceeds with some hysteria but comparatively smoothly as it always does. Anne has prepared most of the food in advance, scraping vegetables, stirring up ingredients to stuff the turkey, baking mince pies and decorating a Christmas cake. She has enjoyed doing it. She feels no resentment as she lights the candles she has placed in the middle of the table.

Anne is clearing away when the sister-in-law she dislikes least comes into the kitchen to ask if she can help. She looks tired. Her flimsy dress is too tight and badly creased. She has spilt some cranberry sauce down the front of it, and the purple stain she has tried to scrub off is clearly visible. Her shoes have already been abandoned in the hall. Anne dismisses her with a smile and her sister-in-law returns to the lounge, to a large glass of wine in front of the television after which she can doze and dream. The volume of the television has been turned up to accommodate Anne's mother. Soon there will be gentle snoring to which Anne's mother herself will eventually contribute.

The children have settled down. Bars of chocolate from their selection boxes lie half eaten around the room with glasses of fizzy pop next to them. Three sweet cigarettes hang from the mouth of Anne's nephew, and her niece pretends to puff away on a liquorice pipe filled with coconut tobacco. The Children's Smoking Sets are doubtful gifts received every year from an aunt the children do not know and have never met. They are highly disapproved of.

Anne counts each plate, bowl, glass, vegetable dish, knife, fork, and spoon while she washes them. When she has a total, she works out exactly how many pieces each person has used.

It is exactly eleven. It pleases her that the total is devisable exactly by the number in the family, with no remainder.

She returns to the lounge. Her book lies on an armchair, and she moves the chair slightly to one side so that the television is not in her eyeline. Duncan has woken up and is lazily pushing dates into his large wet mouth. He looks over at her.

'I see you're reading whatshisname, the one about the flying duck?' He sucks noisily on an unaccustomed cigar. Anne looks up.

'The Snow Goose. Paul Gallico,' she says and looks down again. She has probably been unnecessarily short with him, and he turns to Anne's younger brother Ian, nods his head towards Anne and smirks.

The children have opened a monopoly box and are beginning to arrange the pieces on the table. Their insistent whines bring their parents, Anne, and Anne's mother unwillingly to the table to join the game. Anne sees immediately that there are two few pieces for them all to play. She opens the door and says she is going upstairs for a nap. The others look at her in surprise but with little concern as she leaves the room, closing the door behind her just a little too loudly.

'Something I said?' says Duncan.

'Oh, leave her,' says Anne's mother chewing thoughtfully on a piece of celery she has dipped into a small bowl of salt. 'She was upset about church this morning.' She continues with a cruel breeziness. 'She'll cool down in the water she boiled up in.'

Anne removes her Christmas dress and hangs it up before lying down on the bed. The pillow feels cool against her hot face. She is not exactly unhappy but nevertheless she is starting to wish it was all over. She thinks, not for the first time, how strange it is that she does not feel part of her own family. Temporarily at least, the traditions of their Christmas, like so many before, help her through it. But tomorrow those feelings of not belonging will return. She decides to finish her book and then go back down to cut the Christmas cake.

She looks out of the window and recalls the expression on Barbara West's face when, as a ten- year-old looking out of this same window, Anne had told her that she had seen Santa on his sleigh flying through the sky one Christmas Eve. She remembers the sniggering huddle in the playground looking over at her when Barbara tells the others what she has said.

When she was a child, on Christmas Day afternoon, the whole family sang The Messiah together around the piano, sharing two tattered copies of the music which belonged to her grandparents. Her brothers laugh about it now, but Anne always enjoyed the communal singing. Today the music lay forgotten in a ragged pile beneath the piano stool.

Christmas Day supper was always the highlight of the celebrations. After the over-indulgence, the flushed faces and flatulence, the countless games of Housey Housey, the Tizer on tap, the chocolate cigars and tins of Cadbury's Roses consumed while watching Billy Smart's Circus on the tiny Bakelite television set, the arrival of yet more food in the evening was a family tradition. It would be eaten whether anyone wanted it or not.

Anne remembers it as a remarkable meal not least because the children were allowed to stay up and eat with the adults until way after their bedtime. Fighting heavy eyelids and an overdose of sugar and chocolate, they would go downstairs to the small 'parlour' where miraculously, with the help of an old door balanced across the table and covered in a piece of heavy canvas, twelve people squashed together to eat. Two elderly ladies who lodged in the house next door and who would not have been out of place in a Dickens' novel, always joined them. One sat stiffly at the table, concentrating on her food rather than any frivolous conversation. The other was as round and soft as a ball of wool, her grey felt hat welded to her head throughout the meal. Anne was expected to kiss her when they left. In contrast to her downy cheek, she had a bristly moustache which grazed Anne's lips. The kiss was rather a wet affair and Anne dreaded it.

The tablecloth was turned over to hide the stains of Christmas Dinner. Four brass angels, caught in the heat of four candles underneath, spun dizzily. A plate of white bread was cut into thin slices to ensure there would be enough to go round. It was spread with real yellow butter rather than the usual Summer County margarine. Plates of cold turkey were arranged around the table – dry, pink, tasteless slivers with a small slab of cold stuffing. Left over vegetables were fried off, and the frying pan was placed in the middle of the table. A well-hacked Christmas Pudding followed, with tinned peaches and a family size tin of Carnation evaporated milk. Anne could still hear her mother saying of this treat:

'Well, it is Christmas after all.'

It is different now of course. Anne will soon go downstairs and prepare this meal herself. She thinks about those two elderly neighbours who, like her, were single and childless. They lacked charm or charisma, and that supper was probably the only invitation they received over the Christmas season. The meal itself, tacked on to the end of the festivities before everyone returned to work or school, provided the final opportunity to experience such excess. Anne thinks about this - the people, the food – all left over in some way or other. And now she knows she is joining their ranks.

When she returns to the kitchen, Ian and Duncan are doing what they call 'the men's work.' They are very drunk and chortle stupidly as they carelessly chop up the cooked vegetables and heat oil in a pan. Anne works around them, counting out slices of cold meat and ham, and placing a large loaf of sour dough bread and crisps for the children on the table. An expensive shop-bought cheesecake lies in wait on the counter.

The men whisk plates back and forth in the warm steamy fog which is now filling the kitchen. They throw lumps of cheese to each other to place on the cheeseboard and roar with laughter when a catch is missed; the children are delighted with their fathers' outrageous behaviour. Anne follows them around as unobtrusively as possible, wiping up spillages and putting knives out of harm's way.

The supper of leftovers is crowned with a steaming mountain of bubble and squeak, rising in triumph in the middle of the table. It completely covers the gold Christmas platter, cascading over the edge in places. Glistening brown roasted potatoes and parsnips, mashed green sprouts, bright orange chunks of greasy boiled carrots and the occasional chestnut and butter bean, all fried up - a cornucopia of delight with a hint of dark crispness where something has caught. Jars of chutney stand sentry beside it on one side with a jar of red cabbage on the other.

Anne picks up a jar of small silver-skinned pickled onions, 'angels' eyeballs' her father used to call them. She holds the jar high against the light and counts the shiny little globes carefully. Four each but with one left over (which is a shame.) They make the children's eyes water, and everyone laughs as they bravely crunch away.

For the first time she can remember, Anne's eyes fill with water too. In salty rivulets, it streams uncontrollably down her cheeks and will not stop.

Twitching

Once again, they are spending a damp Bank Holiday Monday in the hide at the local Nature Reserve.

'Look, look…over there…underneath the weeping willow. On that little beach…'

He is whispering urgently, staring intently ahead.

She lifts the binoculars obediently.

'Curlews I think…yes, a pair. Unusual for this time of year.'

She lowers the binoculars and rubs her eyes.

He continues to study the curlews, sitting awkwardly on the hard wooden bench of the hide, oblivious to his surroundings and to her. She takes a small breath.

'There's something I want to talk to you about.'

He cannot take his eyes off the birds and sighs impatiently.

'Not now. Not here. Not in the hide.'

'There's no-one here. Only us.'

He lowers the binoculars and glances down towards her.

'And the birds.' He smiles briefly.

She pulls her coat around her shoulders and carefully fastens each button.

'The swans look so graceful, like galleons in full sail.' She is whispering, apologetic, aware of her clumsy cliché.

'Mmm. So calm and serene above the water. But those great big feet are peddling like mad underneath.' He is happy to continue the cliché. Perhaps he is unaware it is one.

She is silent. And then:

'I need to tell you something really quite important.'

'Oh my God.' He leans forward, binoculars clamped to his face. 'Two pairs of great crested grebes, there, coming out of the weeds. Near that clump of bulrushes… Magnificent.'

He is talking to himself now. 'Apparently, they mate for life. It's probably the same pair we saw here last year…'

She places the binoculars carefully on the ledge below the viewing area. It is sticky with the last occupant's lunch.

'I could do with a coffee.'

'Coffee?' He grunts. 'Not round here. I said you should have brought a flask. You'll have to walk all the way back to the station if you're desperate.'

She pauses.

'I am desperate.'

She picks up her bag.

She opens the wooden door of the hide as quietly as she can, but it creaks as she silently slips outside.

'Bring me one,' he calls after her. 'Make sure it's in a paper cup. And biscuits if they've got any.'

She begins to walk along the muddy path towards the station. It is getting cold now and the sky has started to darken. She ties her scarf round her neck and looks back.

He is still watching the grebes as they swim out of sight on the other side of the lake. The swans turn to watch her as she goes.

Epiphany

She could easily have convinced herself that the whole thing had been an accident. Something over which she had no control. Her visit to the Garden Centre that afternoon, ostensibly to purchase Florentines and some peaches bottled in rum, had undoubtedly ended unexpectedly.

She hoped to find something for Brian there as well. The Guardian puzzle book and green canvas gardening gloves seemed inadequate. It was Christmas Eve, seasonably cold, a light drizzle blanketing coats and hats with a heavy dampness. Inside, the place was crowded, muted excitement enhanced by a band of three mechanical life-size bears bizarrely dressed as tin soldiers 'playing' Christmas songs.

She was the only woman sitting alone in the café. She was wearing her good woollen coat and a scarf with robins on it, in keeping with the occasion. But she was perspiring and regretted the Christmas jumper she wore underneath.

She enjoyed a café, just sitting there, in the middle of a babbling crowd, children red-faced and over-excited. She smiled at anyone who caught her eye and eavesdropped the conversations around her.

She wished she was a writer. Isn't that what writers did? Listened to other people and wrote down what they said. Yes, she should do that. Goodness knows, there was plenty of material all around her.

A man and a woman on the next table were discussing a concert they had attended during which the soprano had provided a particularly forceful version of Ave Maria.

'Not so much Bel Canto as Can Belto,' the man said. They both shouted with laughter, and she wanted to laugh with them.

She looked down at her mince pie. The small lump of brandy butter sat begrudgingly on the edge of her plate, and the sugar holly wreath had broken into several pieces. Her tea was tepid now, but nothing could dent her good humour. She liked being on her own, drinking tea, watching, listening to others. Brian was a pleasant man and not over-opinionated, but he loved to talk about any subject which happened to enter his head, droning on, leaving no gaps for anyone else to contribute. This afternoon was a kind of luxury for her.

In front of her, a child of about five was almost asleep, fairy dress torn and grubby and face covered with sticky pink icing. She pulled at her mother's arm but, oblivious, her mother continued to talk to a group of women laden down with last minute purchases.

She looked down into her bag. She had the peaches and the Florentines and a rather daring French cheese for Brian. The damp was beginning to seep uncomfortably through her coat. Her scarf would not provide any warmth when she went outside. She sighed. She really ought to go.

A loud bell signalled the shop's imminent closure. Crowds drifted towards the exit and in some sections, lights were already dimming. Staff stood sentry by the door, checking their watches, trying not to look impatient. It was early closure on Christmas Eve, and they wanted to get away. She caught the eye of one young man surreptitiously removing his Garden Centre lanyard and smiled sympathetically.

She needed the toilet. Picking up her bag, she walked towards the ladies. It was empty now but as she sat in her cubicle, she heard someone come in and check each cubicle before calling out with a hint of irritation:

'If you could hurry up madam the shop is closing now.' And after a pause: 'Happy Christmas.'

She did not want to hurry up. She would take her time. But just as she was washing her hands, she heard a loud thump and a series of clicks, and the lights went out.

She stood very still in complete darkness. She did not know what to do. She did not go rushing outside or call out to indicate that she was still inside. She just waited.

She could hear cars leaving the car park, music blaring from radios, greetings shouted through open windows. Then - silence.

She knew then that this was what she had been waiting for. They had all gone. And she was still here. She did not feel panicked or frightened. What she felt was a thrill of excitement.

She opened the door of the ladies quietly, afraid there might be an alarm, but perhaps in haste someone had forgotten to set it. Outside the silence was almost palpable. The only light came from a forest of imitation Christmas trees surrounding Santa's Grotto. She looked at them and remembered how as a child, Christmas tree lights were not turned on until Christmas Eve. She would sit and look at them in semi-darkness until it was time for her to go to bed. It was a magical time. But could this be yet another occasion she had misremembered?

She began to wander tentatively around the shop floor. It was strange - how burglars must feel, she thought. Suddenly, she froze. Three security men stood in a row, staring at her at silence. Were they holding guns? Then she realised it was the tin soldier bears, their instruments held out stiffly as if offering her gifts. She laughed out loud.

She continued to explore, keeping away from the windows as she moved around. It was very dark, and the Christmas Trees did not throw out much light. She found a Santa hat with a large red light on top of it and pulled it over her head. At least she could see where she was going now.

It wasn't really a Garden Centre at all. True, there was a small area at the back selling drooping bedding plants and expensive ceramic plant containers, but most of the profits were made here inside. Displays of gaudy Christmas decorations lay next to the Christmas trees, and in one corner, garden furniture and barbecues were being offered in a pre-Christmas sale. Perfumed candles and silver necklaces stood in a cabinet near the tills, and by the café, tables held flavoured fudge and fancy biscuits in front of glass-fronted fridges containing cheese and Cornish cream.

If only I'd known, she thought. I could have taken my time choosing that cheese for Brian. But the fridges were locked, and she thought of Brian again.

What could she do about him? In about an hour, he would start to worry when it was obvious no meal was being prepared. Nothing special tonight even though it was Christmas Eve. She had planned to fill some vol-au-vents with egg mayonnaise and cut some cubes of Cheddar to eat with pickles and crackers in front of the television.

Her heart began to sink. She would have to let him know she was alright. Egg mayonnaise vol-au-vents and Brian's running commentary about the quality of dancing on Strictly held no attractions for her. She wanted to stay where she was.

She began to feel hungry and made her way to the café. Metal shutters had been drawn over shelves displaying fancy foods and bottles of wine, and they were locked. She found a door at the back marked 'Staff Only.' Inside were two small shabby armchairs, a kettle and a small (unlocked!) cupboard containing a few tea bags and a jar of instant coffee. In a tiny fridge she found an almost empty carton of milk and half a bottle of brandy. Wrapped in a muslin cloth on the worktop was half a Christmas cake.

Well, she thought. I've got a feast here. She began to prepare her supper. A sense of well-being enveloped her.

Meagre it may have been, but the food delighted her. She ate a Florentine with a generous slice of Brian's cheese and drank a tot of brandy in the smallest cup she could find. This made her feel sleepy. She thought of Brian again.

She removed her mobile from her bag. It was nearly out of charge, which filled her with a sense of urgency. A text would be easier she thought. She didn't want to upset him unnecessarily though goodness knows this text would upset him enough.

'Don't worry about me. I am well and safe. I need some time alone. You could probably do with that too. Will contact you after Christmas. Sorry about this.' A kiss? No, perhaps not.

She returned to the shop floor. She was very cold now. Her Santa hat light directed her to the women's clothing, where she found a purple quilted coat with a fur collar. Not something she would have bought herself but still…

She moved back to the Christmas trees, collecting a festive tartan dog blanket on the way. In the Sales Section, a garden chair, with a bit of manoeuvring, opened out into a sun lounger. That'll do, she said out loud.

It was probably the most uncomfortable bed she had ever slept on. The only sound was the snuffling in the straw of the guinea pigs and rabbits in the cages behind her. Cardboard angels hung from the ceiling above, their flimsy wings reflecting the light from the Christmas trees. She lit a candle (£20! – who would pay that for a candle?) and its strong smell of incense wafted around the cavernous interior as a distant church bell struck twelve. 'Happy Christmas me,' she said. With the help of more brandy, she closed her eyes and slept.

Christmas Day dawned grim and grey. It was still raining. She had not slept well. The dog blanket lay on the floor, and she was now so cold that she had to scurry over to collect two more. She returned to her makeshift bed and wondered what she should do now.

Daylight obliterated the romance of the night before, but her mood was unchanged. She imagined Brian waking alone, probably worried and wondering what the hell he was going to have for his Christmas Dinner. Well, the food is there she thought. He only needs to put it all together. She knew he would not be able to do that.

She wandered back to the staffroom clutching the dog blankets around her. Daylight enabled her to discover further culinary delights. Two large tins in a cupboard under the sink contained some sausage rolls and three stale mince pies.

Afterwards, she returned to the sun lounger. She made it as comfortable as she could with the addition of some cushions from an indoor gazebo. (Half price! she noted.) Near the jewellery, she found some books including a Sudoko puzzle magazine with a handy Christmas pencil attached. She went back to her bed and settled down.

And there she stayed, dozing fitfully all day but feeling quite content. As the light drained out of the building, she lit the candle again and read until at last, she dropped off to sleep.

She knew the Garden Centre would open for the Boxing Day sales. She needed a plan of action. She woke early, her feet like blocks of ice. She replaced the coat (shame, it was a lovely fit) and most of the blankets. She tidied up the staffroom. And waited.

At eight, with a loud clank of shutters and opening of locks, the manager of the Garden Centre came through the door. He looked around. Everything was as he had left it. He would need to dismantle Santa's Grotto today but that could wait. He went into the staffroom to make tea as more staff arrived.

The elf peering out of Santa's Grotto chose her moment. As soon as all the staff had disappeared, she crept slowly towards the door using the Christmas trees as cover. She made her way to a lone car in the car park.

She would call in and see Brian. She owed him that. But then she would go. Perhaps find that little place she had dreamt about – a small community on a remote Scottish island, where she could do what she liked and be alone? Maybe even, a writing career beckoned?

Belici's Clown

Bridget's life began again with a shabby little café on the main road running away from the heath. It stood between a Turkish Kebab House and Ida's Knits and Bobs, and she spent some time painting the window frames and door a bright yellow. This did little to improve its appearance. But it was hers. Not often had she been able to say that.

The Cross Keys stood opposite. It had been a tired boozer when Bridget opened the cafe but was gradually experiencing something of a reincarnation. One in a row of run-down Georgian houses nearby, just back from the heath, had been purchased by a young couple unable to afford Canary Wharf. Scaffolding had appeared, and passers-by making their way to the heath to walk their dogs, paused to stare as genuine Georgian windows were re-installed, and pots of bay trees were placed on either side of the doorstep.

'It only takes one,' Frank Turner had said to Bridget, and he was right. More houses were purchased and renovated, until the metamorphosis from the wrong to the right side of the heath was complete. Frank enjoyed his unexpected success. Each evening, he leant across the bar relishing the fact that his fortunes had changed, and that his pub was nearly always crowded. His large red face was full of far more bonhomie than Bridget could ever remember.

'It's been a long time coming,' he said to her. 'Yes, a long time coming.'

Sometimes at five o'clock, Bridget would complete her extensive clean-up operation, polishing surfaces and scrubbing pans, then hang up her overall on a hook in the kitchen, lock the door, and make her way across the road to the pub for half a lager. She liked to be alone in a crowd, it didn't matter who they were. She sat at the small table by the door which was usually vacant because of a cutting draft which froze ankles every time the door opened or closed. Sometimes she shared a few words with Frank or Wally, a Local Character who played his guitar occasionally. His 1960s protest songs were incongruous within Frank's new cream walls and bunches of hops and dried herbs which now hung from the ceiling. Bridget noticed that the new set patronised Wally with a cruel glee but gradually he became a quirky addition to their night out at the pub.

Bridget's café had also seen several reincarnations. In those heady yet terrible days when she was acclimatising to her new-found freedom, Ginny, her mother's sister, had found the place and offered to pay the rent for six months. The gesture was as generous as it was unexpected. Bridget did not know and never asked why Ginny had done it because she did not want to hear the reply. Who knew what might come pouring out? Ginny, poor sat-upon Ginny, who had been bullied by her older sister all her life, had been there, had seen what had happened but had never talked to anyone about it after the trial (and barely during the trial as well.) Perhaps it was misplaced guilt? Perhaps she thought she should have done more for Bridget? Bridget did not want to think about any of it.

The café was little more than a Greasy Spoon at first, entirely in keeping with the small row of establishments on that stretch of road. Lorry drivers thundering towards the Blackwall Tunnel were her main source of income. They stopped for bacon sandwiches, a full English, mugs of tea. She liked them. They treated her with friendly respect, and this was new to her. One had even invited her out to watch stock car racing. But she still felt raw and vulnerable. It was one thing chatting over eggs and bacon, but quite another spending a whole evening with one person. She turned him down, but he continued to persist. She was touched that he kept on trying.

After six months she was able to afford the rent without Ginny's help. She felt it was time for a change and Bridget's Café became Bridget's Tea Shop. Losing most of her former customers was unfortunate and quite a gamble but she had become no stranger to risk or fear.

She took on a part-time waitress called Chloe, who had a shaved head, several piercings and enviable confidence. She didn't care much for the customers, but she was reliable and efficient. When St Christopher's Private Day School opened in a large house behind the pub, boarded up for as long as Bridget could remember, her clientele changed. She had just started to become anxious that opening Bridget's Tea Shop had been a step too far and could end in financial disaster. But when term started, groups of mothers began to arrive each morning, just after drop-off. They wore loose duster coats and expensive trainers, shiny well-cut hair hanging around their smooth faces. Designer-clad toddlers fidgeted on their laps while they laughed loudly and talked in shrill north London accents.

'Bloody knobs,' Chloe had muttered under her breath one day. 'So, we don't serve mashed avocado on sourdough. The world won't cave in.'

But that was all it took for Bridget to add it to the menu. She did not approve of private education, but she had a business to run, and the patronage of these women enabled her to keep afloat, to be more adventurous and even eventually, to invest in an eye-wateringly expensive coffee machine. This gleaming work of art produced superior coffee which attracted more customers, most of whom probably had similar machines in their kitchens at home.

Bridget renamed the café 'Coffee on the Heath.' The menu was practically unchanged, but the chintz was replaced by pale blinds, and several vintage mirrors were attached to the walls. The yellow paint went too. Bridget was cautiously optimistic.

'Very nice,' said Frank ostensibly visiting for a coffee. 'Like what you've done.' He studied the décor with the eye of a man who was now an expert in this area. He criticised the coffee from the beautiful new machine, but Chloe said: 'That's only because the coffee he serves at The Cross Keys tastes like gnats' piss.'

Ginny called in occasionally. On her first visit, she looked around and smiled slightly but made no comment. When she chatted with Bridget, Bridget's mother was never mentioned. Soon it was as if her mother had never existed although she continued to lurk around in Bridget's dreams; times and places were vague and confused, and Bridget often woke perspiring heavily. She concentrated on pushing those memories further and further back, as far as she was able. Severe headaches seemed a small price to pay for such selective amnesia.

She did think about Trent Easton, however.

'Trent? What sort of a name is that?' her mother had said and afterwards always referred to him as The American. But for Bridget, sleeping in that tiny box room in her mother's house, working in a dead-end job at the tax office, Trent was the answer to her prayers. And she did pray every night, kneeling bedside her bed like a child, pleading to a God she did not believe in, for something, anything, to come along which would rescue her from the hell of life with her mother.

One gloomy April morning when grey moisture clung to hats and coats, and the atmosphere lowered the spirits, a young man stood uncertainly just inside the door of Bridget's coffee shop. It was always busier on mornings like this. Bridget was serving the last of the school-gate mothers with lattes and croissants. She glanced up and saw him hovering beside a row of damp coats hanging on the back wall, steaming in the warmth of the place. He was clutching a pile of leaflets he had withdrawn from a yellow canvas satchel, and she prepared her usual polite speech explaining that she did not accept publicity shots in the shop.

The man looked around then sat down at one of the tables near the back. The morning rush was beginning to peter out and reluctantly, Bridget approached the table to take his order. She was exhausted, Chloe was sick, and it had been non-stop all week. Without thinking she sat down opposite him.

He was slightly older than she had thought at first, and was hesitant, uncomfortable in what appeared to be unfamiliar surroundings.

'I'm so sorry. We don't take…' She looked down at the leaflets. He leaned forward.

'What about just one in the window, not on every table?'

She recognised a slight accent. Eastern European perhaps? He had an extraordinary face – a long, thin nose which met a firm, generous mouth, and pale blue watery eyes suggesting tears at any moment. But it was his skin which was so striking, soft leather, the texture of a young woman's. She studied him for some time until she knew she could not refuse him. Just this once. The advertisements were for the circus which descended on the heath every Easter for about three weeks. She took a leaflet and promised to attach it to the front window.

Ivor came to the coffee shop almost every day. Sometimes she sat and drank her coffee with him while he sipped hot chocolate like a child, spooning the cream and froth into his mouth. He told her he had to rehearse every morning – he was never sure what part he was to play at the evening's performance. His skills appeared to be manifold - juggling, acrobatics, even trapeze. Bridget said these were exactly the skills she needed to run the coffee shop, but he did not understand what she meant.

Bridget was interested in this exotic life so different from her own. She did not consciously look forward to his visits but listening to him provided opportunities to think about something other than baking scones, making the books balance, and querying the wholesaler's bills. Even though the coffee shop was well-established now, her life had become humdrum. She felt she had little of interest to contribute to their conversations.

'The Belici Brothers?' she said one morning, pointing to the name embroidered on his shirt. 'Where did that come from?'

'Our name is not Belici and we are not brothers,' he said. 'Mr Belici gave us free coffee in his café once for entertaining the customers, just after we arrived in London.'

'That seems a good deal in anyone's money,' she said.

Bridget was charmed by Ivor. He had a fragility, almost a despair, as he talked. He rarely smiled. She wondered if he had ever had much opportunity to talk to anyone outside the circus community. She knew Frank did not welcome those 'bloody circus folk.' Even Ida in the wool shop, kind sweet Ida, spoke of their lifestyle about which she knew absolutely nothing, with mild disdain.

Ivor asked Bridget if she had ever been to a circus. She thought of the annual treat when she had been taken to the circus on the heath by her father. It was almost as thrilling as Christmas. She had loved the horses, the lion-tamer, the performing seals, the magical atmosphere of the Big Top. Her acute fear of clowns had followed her into adulthood. She told Ivor about this, but it was beyond his comprehension how anyone could be afraid of characters who only wanted to make the audience laugh. 'And,' he said staring down into his cup, 'when I perform with the Belicis, I am the clown.'

Ivor gave her two tickets for the final performance. She protested faintly. She explained she had no-one to go with, Chloe would certainly not be interested, and she decided that even if he insisted, she would not go. He looked at her and unexpectedly took her hand.

'Please come. I would like you to see the show. Afterwards you can come round to my wagon. It is dark blue, near the back. It has my name on it.'

He stared at her. She was concerned that the request might contain far more than an invitation to the circus. His expression appeared to suggest something else entirely. The back of her throat constricted and there were stirrings deep in the pit of her stomach. She had not felt like this for some time.

A long queue was forming outside the circus tent as she approached across the muddy grass. Red and yellow lights shone across the heath and children waved twinkling windmills, screaming with excitement when one of the performers walked by. She waited in line and once inside was shown to her seat by one of the dreaded clowns who sprayed red paper confetti at the audience as she made her way to her seat. He turned to stare at her with small black eyes above a large red nose and whitened face. Clowns like him still had the power to make her uneasy.

She knew there would be no animals, but she was not prepared for the music which made her ears throb, and the strobe lighting whizzing backwards and forwards across the audience and out of the Big Top into the night sky. This razzamatazz accompanying every act was met with a wall of noise from the audience. An abrasive tannoy system, so loud that announcements were distorted, could not have been more different from the cries of the top-hatted ringmaster. Cheap furry toys were flung out to children in the audience, a poor replacement for the performing dogs who balanced balls on their noses and scampered around in their frilled collars and tiny hats. The shining white dancing horses with gold and silver plumes, cantering around the ring while acrobats jumped from back to shimmering back, had been replaced by screeching gun-metal go-carts which careered dangerously up and down an insubstantial-looking wall erected so near the audience, a fatal accident seemed inevitable.

And then the dreaded clowns appeared. There seemed to be hundreds of them, surrounding Bridget, threatening, and mocking. The noise reached a climax of impossible volume and there, rearing up behind the clowns' manic grins, she saw her mother's face. Her mouth was wide open in a perfect O as she screamed silently down at her.

Bridget's head was on fire and exploded with memories she longed to suppress. More pictures flashed before her. Her mother's face like thunder when she failed the 11+, lips tight across her teeth. Her mother sneering at her boyfriends – uncouth, too mouthy, unpolished shoes. Her mother informing her that Trent needed a woman with more upstairs in the brains department. Her mother's triumph at a family tea when she announced that The American had left Bridget because he couldn't hold an intelligent conversation with her. 'I said to you Ginny, didn't I? I said this won't last.' Now Bridget saw the salad Aunty Ginny had brought - the tired lettuce, the stringy celery, the two radishes staring gloomily up at her. She remembered how her heart pounded as it was doing now, the rush of blood when she picked up the bread knife and lunged towards her mother. She saw again the red wetness at the back of her mother's dentures, and the bright puddle of blood creeping slowly across the white Sunday-best tablecloth as her mother slumped forward. She heard Ginny's scream, saw her rush from the room. And now, in time with the harsh rhythm of the circus music, she found herself whispering: 'I *meant* to do it, I *meant* to do it,' over and over again. She knew that now.

Bridget opened her eyes. She felt wrung out and was quietly weeping when Ivor came prancing into the ring. With glittering face and hair, she hardly recognised him. He was wearing dark blue tights which accentuated his thin childlike legs, and a spangled shirt with flowing sleeves caught at the wrist. On his feet, strange little flat shoes reminded her of school plimsolls. She watched him leaping over other members of the acrobatic troupe and balancing on their shoulders. Her emotions were all over the place but looking at Ivor, she felt something akin to embarrassment and even pity. It brought with it a great shame she could not explain.

Afterwards Bridget made her way along the row of unstable wooden seats, treading over half-eaten hot dogs, cardboard cups, and the occasional beer can. She was still shaking. It was cold and misty outside, and the circus lights lit the foggy sky. They had suggested so much - the 'thrills and spills' described on the poster. But the experience she had had inside, had little to do with the circus itself.

Disappointment overcame her. She remembered the suggestion in Ivor's voice, the slight leer on his handsome face when he had invited her to his wagon. She had dressed carefully, worn make-up for the first time in years but now her face was grubby and tear stained. That she was a silly old woman taken in by a handsome face might become an amusing anecdote she would share with Chloe and Ida one day. She felt some affection for Ivor, was almost grateful to him. But she was glad the circus was leaving tomorrow. She did not want to see him again.

It was the promise of the circus itself which had let her down. It was not what she had expected, not what she remembered. She wished she had not come. She had hoped it would conjure up happy memories of being with her father, but instead it had triggered the worst possible memories, ones she had tried to bury for so long.

She turned off the path and made her way across the heath. She could just see the coffee shop in the distance. In her haste she stumbled on a large grassy hillock she had not seen in the dark. But she recovered herself and avoided falling into the mud in front of the large departing crowd.

Un Sac de Malice

Iris crawled out of the girls' toilets into the playground. She stood up and studied her legs where damp grit was embedded in her knees. Slowly she made her way to the school gates. She needed to get home, to wrap herself in a cocoon of sheets beneath the blankets on her bed. Her school skirt was torn in the front - her mum would go mad when she saw it. She would not care how it had happened. Her teachers would never believe her. Why would they? It was so terrible it was barely believable.

It dawned on her slowly. She began to think that if such a thing could happen to someone like her, what was the point of being a good girl who worked hard at school? She may as well behave however she liked and do as little as she could possibly get away with.

The small pellet of plasticine hit Mam'selle square on the back of her neck. It stung even though she knew it would happen sooner or later. Iris, hardly her most attentive pupil, had constructed a catapult out of drinking straws and an elastic band, and was shooting missiles around the room when her back was turned.

There could be nothing worse than trying to teach a group of recalcitrant teenage girls on a sweltering Friday afternoon in July. Poor Mam'selle. Her olive skin had a sallow translucence which gave her face an expression of inevitable defeat. The arid atmosphere was heavy with pupil boredom and there was no way she could make the lakes and rivers of France sound sexy. The girls wanted to escape for cigarettes and gossip, a desire with which she sympathised.

Her exasperation reached its limit and the class watched with delight when she cried out: 'Iris, vous êtes un sac de malice.' In front of her, she saw a sullen sea of incomprehension. She took some chalk and scrawled the sentence across the board. Malice! They liked that. The class giggled but Iris didn't care. She draped herself across her desk not even trying to suppress a yawn. She began embellishing with hearts and daggers the initials of her latest pash which she had creatively inked on the front of her French exercise book. She recalled how yesterday he had chosen her to accost out of so many other girls at the bus stop, and how he had stolen two of her lemon fancies from the Tupperware box she was carrying home after double cookery. How the others stared with envy.

Iris adjusted her pleated skirt, rolled several times over its waistband, and frilling out like a crooked lampshade. Attempting to replicate a Sassoon bob, she had cut her hair with nail scissors, and now a wonky fringe fell over one eye. Against school rules, she wore two pairs of false eyelashes and a heavy layer of American Tan foundation. Only that morning the deputy head, who was well acquainted with Iris and should have known better, had smeared her finger across Iris's cheek, examined it, and enquired: 'Do I detect a matt finish?' Iris had laughed and skipped away.

Her ability to annoy teachers had flowered recently. She discovered she had quite a talent for it. But malice? She had no idea it translated as 'mischief.' She much preferred malice.

While Iris chattered James's irritation grew, manifesting itself through grunts and monosyllabic responses. He rarely contributed to a conversation unless he had initiated it, and now he placed his knife and fork carefully down on to his plate. Iris should have seen the signs.

'D'you know Iris, you haven't said one positive thing all night?' he said. 'You've been vile about everyone. It's tedious to listen to. And actually, just plain nasty.' His voice was dangerously calm. Iris twisted her napkin around her fingers, aware she should heed the warning. Instead, she was mildly defensive.

'It's just a bit of harmless gossip James. Come on. There's no malice in it.'

James leaned forward, closing his eyes and raising his eyebrows in a way guaranteed to get under her skin. With patient disapproval he said:

'But there is. It's all malicious. You say such terrible things. Isn't there anyone you like? Anyone you admire?'

Iris looked down at her plate.

James, a devout Catholic who attended Our Lady of Perpetual Succour twice a week, was wearing the pious expression usually reserved for his return from mass. His religious zeal extended to a Friday night ritual of cooking fish for supper, frowning as he filleted or fried, boiled or baked. Initially Iris had found this endearing. But only initially.

Tonight, a bright pink salmon stared up at her sadly, untouched, and sweaty. A familiar confusion washed over her.

'It's not always easy to be positive,' she said.

'Clearly not.' His voice rose a little. 'Why is it so hard? You have everything you want.' He turned to look out of the window. 'Sometimes I think I really don't know you at all.'

'No' she replied. She felt flat, without energy. 'I don't think I really know myself.'

It was not the first time James had accused her of gossiping. Inexplicably, her interest in the foibles and failings of others provided her with a rush of pleasure which James did not share. She looked up at the jars, tins and cannisters arranged on a shelf. If he could, James would have coloured-coded them or put them in alphabetical order, but he could not countenance the chaos of mixing savoury and sweet. Once he had organised them in size order and when he was out Iris had taken pleasure in moving them around. It was a pyrrhic victory. When he returned, he moved them back again without comment, a martyr to her childish action.

After the meal, they moved around each other in silence. Nothing more was said. This was depressing but not unusual. Most evenings James found things to do which did not include her. She had discovered some time ago that this was not necessarily a bad thing.

Iris sat very still for a full five minutes before starting the car. The sweat on her face had cooled unpleasantly and her breathing was quick and shallow. Too late she thought of what she might have said, the witty quips effecting a careless air of feigned forgetfulness. She certainly would not have worn baggy tracksuit bottoms and a green matted jumper. Dangly earrings and a spikey haircut may have given her the courage to say what she had been rehearsing for years. Her oatmeal jacket would have been good too although the stains of vomit on the front would have been more difficult to remove than those she stared down at now.

Forty minutes ago. Was that really all it was?

A Spring sun radiated unseasonal heat. In the carpark, drivers jostled for spaces, bobbing up and down over the top of their steering wheels like indignant meercats. Inside the supermarket, the white lights and freezing temperature in the first aisle were oppressive. Automatically she placed cheese, cold meat, butter, and juice into her trolley. She remembered she had even been humming.

The man was standing in front of a shelf displaying special offers, inspecting the label on an out-of-date packet of prawns. He looked awkward; Iris slowed and turned to stare at him. There was something about the way he dropped his head from rounded shoulders, the way he rocked forward on to the balls of his feet. A significant beer belly protruded from an unbuttoned wool shirt. His legs, encased in tight black trousers, were thin and slightly bowed. He had brushed his hair back from his face and thick hair oil gave him an unkempt appearance.

Sensing that Iris was staring at him, he looked up. He began to smirk. Did he recognise her as well? His fleshy lips drooped beneath a large glistening nose and although clean-shaven, his pallor was grubby. She imagined his fingernails caked with dirt. He looked the type.

Iris experienced a sharp physical reaction. Apprehension rose from her stomach like bile. He made no move to get out of her way when she began to manoeuvre her trolley around him. His eyes narrowed and disappeared into folds of pasty flesh just above his cheekbones. He smiled broadly.

'It can't be! Little Iris Rowland!' She thought he spoke with the joviality of an abattoir butcher.

'Sorry, your name's gone.' Apologetically, she tapped her forehead with her finger, despising herself for the pretence. He grinned at the lie.

'Come on Iris. It's me, Fraser Leavis. 4L – Mrs Longmore's class. You must remember! I sat behind you. You called me a bloody pest once!' Thirty years ago. He was on safer ground now.

A bloody pest. Oh, Fraser Leavis you were so much more than that. Two years older than all the other children in the class (why was that? - no-one ever explained), he was tall and physically threatening. She closed her eyes briefly and then rubbed them with her thumbs so that he would not see she was near to tears. Here was the reason why that last year at primary school had become a terrifying blur. Here. Standing right in front of her.

The sensation of purple paint blown through a straw into her hair and then dripping down her cheek in blood-like rivulets. The cold metal of blunt school scissors pulling and snipping away at her hair until one plait was significantly shorter than the other. The sharp compass point scratching around her earlobe until she wished he would just pierce it and get it over with. The salty smell of hot breath, and spit dripping down her back. Rough sweaty hands easing round her neck. And the other things…

She had always believed it must have been her fault. What other explanation could there be? Of course, she didn't think that now. But there in the supermarket talking - *talking!* - to Fraser Leavis, she felt frantic with panic and an anger she could barely contain.

'You local?' His tone was friendly, conversational. He took a step towards her. She flinched. His basket barred her way, and she had an urge to jump into the middle of it, smashing the beer bottles, exploding the eggs, causing a stir. She looked down and pretended to give her shopping list a cursory glance.

'I've just moved in round the corner,' he said, unaware of her discomfort. 'A starter home! At my age!' He laughed unpleasantly. Everything he said or did now was unpleasant.

'That's nice,' she said. He was to be her neighbour. She might have to meet him again and again. How could she bear it? She pushed her trolley forward slightly.

'Well, I've got to get going or I'll be late.' Another lie, not lost on him. She took a deep breath and clutched her trolley to still her trembling hands. 'Goodbye.'

He did not reply. She reversed her trolley away from him and wheeled it swiftly back the way she had come. She knew he was watching her go. Abandoning the trolley outside the ladies, her fingers were still shaking as she unhooked her empty shopping bags and made her way outside. She hoped Fraser had not followed her. She could not locate her car keys and when she did, she could not fit them into the door. She almost fell into the driver's seat.

Quite suddenly she vomited. She scrabbled around in the glove compartment for some tissues and found an old cloth she used to wipe the windows. She scrubbed at her jumper and stared helplessly at her pale face in the mirror. Self-pity made her cry. A woman wheeling her trolley past stared at her, but she did not stop.

Iris had hoped Fraser Leavis was fading from her memory but in one fell swoop, here he was again. When she was eighteen, she had developed a terrible obsession about him. He had become an amateur country and western singer and she had followed his whereabouts in venues across the East Midlands. She had even been to one of his 'performances' in the cellar of an old Miners' Welfare Club in Blidworth. She had hidden in the shadows biding her time but had failed to find the courage to run on the stage and tell the audience what he had done to her when she had been at primary school.

Iris could hear James's monotonous voice worming its way into her head. Think positive thoughts, Iris. Breathe, and think positive thoughts. Well, fuck you, she thought. You have no bloody idea what I've just been through. It felt good to blame him.

At home, James met her wearing his gardening clothes – an expensive sweater which the moths had got at and misshapen jeans which sagged around his thin bottom. He did not ask her where the shopping was but sighed and folded his lips across his teeth. He said he would coddle himself an egg. Iris bristled at the word – no-one coddled eggs in her house when she was a child. However, she did not have to suffer his 'coddling egg' lecture tonight; she was well versed in the importance of discarding an egg which sank below the surface of the boiling water because it was not fresh. Positive thoughts, Iris. Positive thoughts.

'Did you remember Ginny's soiree tomorrow night?' said James, coddling away by the stove. 'A new beau I think.' He did not offer to prepare food for her.

Iris was disinclined to tell him about her meeting with Fraser. She felt she ought to but walked away from him with the weight of unsaid things settling firmly in her throat. She stared out of the window. The sky had not yet darkened. She could just make out the profiles of late daffodils and early tulips.

A few months earlier, Iris's desire for a child had gradually started to grow but James dismissed the idea with a mocking laugh. He said their lives were good - he had his running club and canasta games with the boys, she had the house and her book club. Why rock the boat? Their sex life was good, wasn't it? Wasn't it? Did they really need a child? Yes, Iris screamed silently. But it was another subject which was not mentioned again.

Preparing for the soiree neither wanted to attend, Iris watched James. He stood in his shirt and socks, rifling through neatly arranged clothes in his wardrobe. Her first impression of him five years before – distant, non-committal, grey – had been an accurate one. She had empathised with his post-divorce loneliness; she was lonely herself. Eventually a barely discernible spark ignited between them but the decision to marry was over-hasty, followed by the impulsive purchase of this cottage. Iris was reasonably content at first even though she knew neither of them worked hard enough to make the marriage work. They were too tired of trying now. Looking at him in the mirror, she wondered if they had ever really desired each other.

Ginny was an old friend of James's. Tonight, Iris would have to deal with Ginny's amusing anecdotes, her round pink face and perfectly veneered teeth. Ginny knew everyone. She had read their books, attended their concerts, hung their paintings. Her friends were Trevor-Benson-the-head-of-spinal-surgery-at-Barts or Dame-Helen-Morris-head-of-the-facultyof-law-at-Kings. After an evening in Ginny's company, Iris felt inadequate and frayed. There was rich material for gossip here of course but she had no-one with whom to share it.

Lights shone from every room in Ginny's house, and candles flickered in jam jars at the side of the paved path. Framed within the glazed porch Ginny, ever the retired ballerina, stood with feet in fourth position. She wore a strange silk kaftan with matching scarf wound tightly around her head. Meeting Iris's eyes, she pouted and smiled as James provided the expected kiss on both cheeks.

Tonight, Iris had decided to show James her positive side. No nasty comments, no ridiculing Ginny's outfit (though heaven knows that was going to be difficult), no making fun of Ginny's incomprehensible ceramic sculpture collection scattered around in the lounge. There, small clumps of guests were attempting conversation above the music but with so few of them, a party atmosphere was difficult to create.

Iris was hungry. She wondered whether a 'soiree' was a polite way of saying no food would be provided? James wandered off to find drinks. Iris removed her jacket and turned to look through a glass partition into the kitchen. Ginny was drying glasses with a white tea towel, gazing up at a tall man beside her who was drinking from a brown leather tankard. Iris was immediately scathing about the tankard but then she stopped to stare. Surely, surely this was not Ginny's new man?

James returned to find Iris scrabbling for car keys in her handbag. He offered her some wine and, misreading the situation, said:

'Look, we don't have to stay. Just one drink. No-one'll notice.'

But it was too late. Fraser was looking straight at her and had begun moving across the room. There was no escape – no trolley to hide behind, no excuses about an appointment she did not have. James had turned away to speak to one of his canasta pals. Fraser stopped in front of her and grinned.

'Fraser Leavis again.' He gave a mock salute. 'Remember me this time?' He was laughing at her. She thought of him in the supermarket, smug, comfortable in his own skin. She began to tremble, aware of the heat under her arms and on her face. She breathed in.

'Of course I remember you,' she said. She was holding her wine glass far too tightly. 'Blowing paint into my hair, cutting bits off my plaits, spitting down my back. How could I ever forget such a sweet little boy?' She laughed mirthlessly but she was pleased with her performance so far. He moved his face closer, straining to hear what she was saying. He grimaced, an amused sneer curling at the corner of his mouth.

'Little buggers, weren't we?' He looked around. 'Best keep that to yourself. Not something I'd want Ginny to hear about!' He was actually amused! A wave of fury unsteadied her.

'No, I'm sure,' she said. 'And she might not want to hear about the other thing, you know…' His smile faded a little, unsure where this was going. He took a swig from his tankard.

'That sounds ominous.' He placed the tankard on a small table. The room was filling up and Iris kept her voice low. She was on an unfamiliar roll and felt dizzy.

'Do you remember the girls' toilets in the playground?' she said pleasantly. 'God, they were disgusting, weren't they? Freezing and always smelly. I never wanted to use them. I was always desperate for a pee by the time I got home.'

'Yeah. I remember dashing in and out of them when we were playing kiss chase.' Fraser smiled. The threat had passed.

'Oh, I think you were better acquainted with them than that.' Looking into his face, Iris almost lost her nerve. 'There was that cubicle at the end. Bigger than the rest. It was the only one with a lock. D'you remember it?'

'No, I don't!' Laughing with uneasy indignation, Fraser held up his hands palms outwards to protect himself against her words.

'Oh, you must do.' Iris sounded surprise. 'You caught me in there once. Well twice actually. Surely you remember that?'

'Maybe,' said Fraser slowly. 'That vile little gang of ours! Wouldn't be allowed to behave like that today!' He looked away, then back at her and laughed. 'I do remember we all thought you were up for it though.' He looked at her closely to gauge her reaction, wondering if he had gone too far.

'Up for it? Up for what?' Iris's voice was barely a whisper.

'You know.' He grinned. 'Up for a bit of a feel in the toilets. We used to have bets on it.'

'Bets?' Iris stared at him. 'Bets on what?'

'I think I won an elastic snake belt from Gary Harris that day. I was chuffed.' He laughed again but with less confidence. 'Come on Iris. It was nothing. We were just kids. And you were always such a bloody goody-goody. I remember there were extra points for undoing a couple of buttons or putting a hand in your knickers.' He roared with laughter. 'No harm done.'

Iris paused, unable to move. Her confidence was ebbing away.

'But you could see I was terrified. You wouldn't stop, even when I started crying and you got out that stupid little Swiss army knife you carried around with you. That floor was stinking wet.' Fraser stopped laughing and looked at her in silence.

'Hey Iris. Not clever making those kinds of accusations.'

'It's OK,' said Iris. 'I never told anyone. Not even when you caught me for another go.'

'I didn't…'

'Yes, you did.' Iris brought her face closer to his. Her breath was ragged. She found it difficult to speak but she was now filled with a wild energy and knew she had to go on. 'Even worse the second time. Got my knickers off completely and all in front of an audience. Encouraged them all to have a feel didn't you?'

Fraser picked up his leather tankard. He shook his head slowly.

'I've never forgotten it. And I'll never forgive you.'

Iris turned to find James and Ginny standing behind them. Ginny was staring at her. Iris walked past them, collected her jacket from the back of the chair where she had left it, and walked out of the house.

James glanced at her several times on the way home. He tried to take her hand, but she clung to the door handle with her back to him. She ran into the kitchen and sat down at the table, her handbag overturning and spilling its contents with a clatter on to the red tiles. James brought her a brandy in one of the showy balloon glasses they never used. He reached for her fingers but she pulled back and would not look at him.

'How much…?' she said at last. She ran her finger around the rim of the green dish which held their keys.

'Enough,' he said. There was another silence.

'Why didn't you tell me? I had no idea you even knew him.' Iris was silent.

'Ginny's been bending my ear all night about how wonderful this Fraser is. She'll be devastated.'

Iris turned to him slowly, her voice quiet and incredulous. '*She'll* be devastated?'

'Oh God, I'm sorry. This must be terrible for you.' He paused. 'Didn't you ever tell anyone?' His tone became almost challenging. A familiar vulnerability overcame Iris.

'I was ashamed,' she said. 'Embarrassed. I'd rather have died than tell mum and dad.'

'Well, you should have.' He was firmer now, almost chastising her. 'Look, you must go to the police. You must. Tell them what happened.' As an afterthought he added: 'I'll come with you.'

Iris sighed and sat back in her chair.

'I can't bear to think about it, let alone talk to anyone else. And anyway, it happened years ago.'

'They need to know. It's affected you in so many ways.' She would have liked to have asked him exactly what he meant by this, but he blundered on.

'I could kill him. I really could.' Could you? she thought. Could you really? I doubt that. She wanted him to hold her, stroke away her tears, but he was determinedly one-tracked. She said she would never go to the police. After a while he sighed, stood up, and left the room.

Two weeks later Iris sat in the kitchen watching her coffee go cold. James had gone to visit his mother, but Iris was not up to listening to her acerbic 'wit' or witnessing her unconditional love for him. When he returned clutching a madeira cake his mother had made, he was short with her as if she had used up all the sympathy to which she was entitled.

Iris did not regret what she had said to Fraser. In fact, she felt quite exhilarated when she thought about it. But it had triggered unpleasant memories. The deterioration of her behaviour at school, her anxious parents summoned to appear before the head teacher. No-one could explain the dramatic change in Iris, why learning new things no longer enthralled her. She would not answer their questions. It was too much. But when she had seen Fraser again, standing there looking so pleased with himself, something had shifted.

James and Iris were eating trout with almonds one Friday evening when a particularly brutal attack on a fifteen-year-old schoolgirl was announced on the local news. Iris stopped eating. She placed her fork on her plate and sat very still.

'That's near where you run isn't it?' she said. 'Did you see anything?'

'Not on the way there. But there was plenty of police activity on the way back. I did tell you.' He listened to the rest of the report but continued to eat. She knew what he was thinking.

'Funny how something like this happens just after he comes back on the scene,' he said.

'I can't just accuse him,' she said.

'Of course not. But you can report an assault. They'd be able to talk to him at least.' With great precision, he peeled back the skin of his trout. Iris pushed her plate away.

'Another reason not to have kids I suppose,' he said. Iris looked up sharply.

'What the hell do you mean by that?'

'Well, things like this happening. Makes you think.'

'What, we didn't have a child in case she was attacked when she was fifteen?'

'We didn't have a child because you were too old.'

Ah, there it was. After all this time. Iris stared bleakly out of the window.

'I was forty. Well and healthy.'

'Yeah. But still too old I think.'

'We didn't have a child because you didn't want one,' she said. It was a tired argument.

'Not true.' He continued to dissect his trout extracting tiny bones and placing them neatly on the side of his plate.

'Turns out my eggs weren't fresh, was that it? They bubbled beneath the surface and needed to be discarded.'

'Don't be so childish Iris. I would have been nearly sixty when the child went to school, you would have been fifty. I'm happy as I am. I don't need children to feel fulfilled, to take over my life, to bleed me dry…'

'*You* don't need…' Iris stopped. James sighed and took her hand.

'Look, try and be positive. Get down to the police station and tell them about Fraser. You can't carry this around with you forever.' He took his plate to the sink.

'And.' He looked over his shoulder at her. 'We need to consider Ginny's safety.' He walked into the lounge and closed the door.

Well, that's new, thought Iris. Concern about Ginny's safety.

At that moment she disliked him more than she had ever disliked anyone. Slowly she picked up his glass and snapped off the stem, laying it carefully on the draining board and drying her hands on a tea towel. She knew she had to do something before she went mad. She *would* go to the police tomorrow. Inform them of the facts, not her suspicions. It would be up to them to investigate and make connections. That's what they did didn't they? So that she wouldn't have to.

The police arrived at half past three on Wednesday afternoon. The warm weather had broken into a series of angry little showers. Thick cloud cast a grey light on the garden where James was bent over planting late Spring bulbs. Iris, sitting at the table in the kitchen, did not move. She heard James return to the house, the sound of quiet voices in the hall, and then the click as James took his coat from the hook behind the door. He called out to her, but she did not reply. She heard the front door close and the police car drive away. It was calmly and quietly executed.

Iris sat at the table for some time.

In the end his nocturnal activities had enabled her to perform the ultimate act of malice and treachery. James was now lodged beneath the same stone as Fraser Leavis. Such corrosive negativity throughout her life she thought, and it had come to this.

Thoughts drifted in and out of her head. She could make little sense of them. Finally she picked up her car keys from the green bowl and held them so tightly that they marked the palm of her hand. It wasn't too late. She would go to the park and watch the children play.

Casual Damage

In fact, Jo did see Lydia again but not until five years later. She was in a small pub in the Charing Cross Road, hot and noisy, the mirrors behind the bar cloudy with conversation and condensation, and the brass faux-antique lamps shining a dull yellow.

Clearly chosen for its theatrical impact, Lydia was sitting alone at a table, a single light shining down on her face. She was looking down at the large glass of red wine in front of her, tracing its pink reflection on the table with her finger. Jo studied her closely from a position near the bar, unsure whether it really was her.

Lydia was wearing a sleeveless linen dress, seasonably unsuitable but striking, and attracting glances from others in the room. Her face had become jowly but remained arresting. Although her forehead was smooth there were tiny lines around her mouth and eyes, and her hair, well cut and expensively coloured, was a darker shade of red than Jo remembered. It hung casually unbrushed around her face.

Lydia looked up and her eyes met Jo's. She frowned uncertainly. Then she jumped up and began to push through the crowd, smiling, charmingly apologetic.

'It's you!' she said standing back and holding Jo by the shoulders, her pleasure almost genuine. Jo smiled but said nothing. Lydia began to talk as if it were weeks rather than years since they had last seen each other. She pressed Jo for information about her marriage (Jo suspected she was well-aware she did not have one now), and her career in teaching. It was all both faintly insulting but very reminiscent.

'Beautiful dress,' was all she could manage.

'This? I can hardly get into it these days.' She smoothed her hand over a flat stomach. It was not a subconscious movement; Lydia never did anything subconsciously. Jo wanted her to stop talking as she continued to extract details of Jo's life rarely shared with others. Same old Lydia. She did not talk about prison and how it had impacted on her, or what she was doing alone in this pub. At one point she put her head on one side in a familiar gesture and asked about Steve. She appeared to be glad that Jo had no news. Lydia recalled her brief relationship with him. She even touched on the disastrous holiday in France and spoke about it with fondness.

By now Jo could barely speak. With a coquettish giggle Lydia shared some college anecdotes which still amused her. Jo wanted to hit her. Physically hurt her. Her beauty and spite were undiminished, yet both had a sharper edge and Jo needed to get away from Lydia as fast as she could. Perhaps her poison was catching? Perhaps it always had been. Jo was afraid it had poisoned her.

Lydia did not mention the one event which had shaped and twisted Jo's memories of college days. Lydia was the only one who knew what had happened that night. Jo wanted to ask her if she ever thought about it? Ever thought about him? The question remained stuck somewhere at the back of her throat.

Jo lied about a train she had to catch. Neither suggested they meet again. Jo reached the door and turned. Lydia was walking back towards her table, gesturing to the barman for more wine. Perhaps she was a regular here who always drank alone? Jo opened the door and went out into the chilly night. She did not look back.

The first time Jo saw Lydia was at a college lecture one Friday afternoon eight years before. The lecture hall was dark and drowsily warm, and Jo sat with a notebook on her lap. But no-one seemed to be writing anything down except a young man with a glum face sitting on the front row. Jo's seat made no allowance for leg length or bottom width and creaked loudly whenever she moved. She sat up stiffly, unable to retrieve her mobile which she was sure was not on silent. She felt a spasm of fear that it might ring at any minute and her face became hot. Her back and her head began to ache simultaneously. She could just see her quiche-for-one in its dimpled covering peering out of her bag. She hoped this would all end soon.

At last, the lecturer invited questions. He was not encouraging. His tone implied that like most of those present, he wanted to get away as quickly as possible. There was a ripple of annoyance around the hall when a girl with red hair, her college lanyard dangling between her fingers, raised her hand. She spoke out in a clear entitled voice.

'How does the overall premise of your argument tally with R S Peters' views about the philosophy of education?'

The lecturer stared glassily at a spot just above the girl's shoulder. There was some fidgeting around the hall. He was confident that few, except this wretched girl, had ever heard of R S Peters, and regretted stepping in at the last minute to deliver this bloody lecture. He had hoped the notes which had served him well for the past four years would suffice. He consulted the scrawled handwriting on the pages in front of him.

'Well,' he said at last. 'That would be a subject for a whole series of lectures and there's no time for that I'm afraid.' He smiled weakly and began to gather his papers together.

The girl appeared to be satisfied and looked around her with a smile. She had caught him out, and everyone knew it.

As the lights came up, some students gazed around sleepily while others with buses to catch crammed IPads and notebooks into their rucksacks and made for the exit without quite pushing others out of the way. Jo watched the hall empty, the rows shedding their careless occupants who left behind the flotsam and jetsam of student paraphernalia on their seats.

The girl with red hair, one of the last to leave, stood up. She pushed books and her phone into a long, crocheted bag hanging from her shoulder. On her face a small smile remained. It was a minor triumph but triumph it was. What a fool that lecturer was, she thought, delighted to be the cause of his discomfiture.

A cold gritty wind stung Jo's cheeks as she walked head down across the campus. A recent haircut had left her ears exposed and as the freezing air hit them, they rang. She could not remember much about the lecture except disconnected scraps of information, and the question asked by the girl with the red hair. Her first lecture at the college had not been an unqualified success.

Back in her room in halls, her fur slippers lay beside the bed like two slumbering guinea pigs. She filled the kettle without taking off her coat. From the shared kitchen above, she could smell chips fried in old fat, and pizza with too much pesto. She took the quiche from her bag. It did not look quite so appealing now.

The girl with red hair returned to the room someone had arranged for her in an old house on the main road. It was large, brown, and shabbily furnished, but she did not care. It was just a room, and she did not plan to be in it much. It provided a place where she could be alone, and not pestered by those bloody girls she had encountered at the college, screaming and giggling in the girls' toilets or crying tragic tears of homesickness. She had met girls like this many times before although this lot were a good deal more annoying with their little yelps of excitement as they experienced yet another aspect of their new-found independence. She could not relate to this and anyway, she could not have cared less.

Jo was eating breakfast in the refectory the following morning. The girl with the red hair was wandering around and eventually sat down at Jo's table. She peered into her crocheted bag and withdrew a grapefruit and some Greek yoghurt. The egg and beans congealing on a plate in front of Jo looked unappetising, but she was hungry. The girl watched her eat with amusement then leant back and sighed.

'Couldn't face the full fry up,' she said. 'D'you fancy some grapefruit?' Jo said she would rather suck a crate of lemons. The girl laughed.

'I'm Lydia,' she said, not looking up as she spooned yoghurt from the pot. She did not ask Jo her name and Jo did not volunteer it.

Lydia had lightly freckled skin and an unusual face which somehow lacked symmetry. Her mouth was large, and her expression was one of sophisticated cynicism. Her red hair hung heavily, almost to her shoulders. She was physically striking, heavy-limbed, the muscles at the top of her arms well-developed.

Lydia continued to eat her yoghurt and looked around the refectory with little interest. Jo did not like her much and felt awkward. She continued to eat her meal in silence until Lydia suddenly turned and, with chin in hand, began to ask her questions. Staring into her face, Jo was impressed with Lydia's unconventional beauty. She did not understand how Lydia persuaded her to reveal so much about herself. Lydia volunteered very little and dismissed Jo's enquiries with a wave of her hand. Jo didn't care much. She wanted someone to go drinking with. She didn't need to know their life history to do that.

During the first few weeks, when friendships were formed, accepted or rejected, Lydia drifted in and out of Jo's life. If they happened to meet, they might go for a walk on the beach or drink rough cider in the old pub by the docks. Lydia was already an unreliable friend and Jo learned neither to welcome nor miss her.

Lydia was studying art and was already acquainted with students from the art college in town. They had flair, look-at-me self-confidence, in their paint-spattered velvet jackets, enormous woollen jumpers which flapped around their knees, and odd little hats with feathers and seashells pinned to them. Lydia did not particularly like them, but they provided her with drugs and alcohol and took the kind of risks she appreciated. Jo knew she was not edgy enough for these colourful butterflies and anyway considered them the very definition of pretentiousness. She felt out of step, out of kilter when she was with them. Her obvious loathing seemed to please Lydia.

Jo started college at the same time as Steve, an old boyfriend of her sister's. He was older than her, deceptively mild-mannered with a spiteful sense of humour which she suspected Lydia would enjoy. She delayed introducing them. In late October, after an afternoon of whispered jokes and endless bags of Maltesers in the library, Steve asked Jo if she was going to watch the band that night. She smiled casually but felt confused. She was not good at detecting signs.

In front of the forests of arms playing air guitar near the band, Lydia and Steve began dancing together and Jo sighed. She knew this was bound to happen. She could see Lydia putting her head on one side, opening her eyes wide, and listening carefully to everything he said. She had his attention, and she reeled him in.

Jo returned to the bar for more cheap gin. Coming from a family where drinking alcohol was considered the devil's own work, this was an opportunity not to be missed. At midnight she could not even see Lydia and Steve and wandered home alone.

The next day, Lydia woke with a headache. A thin slice of late Autumn sunshine penetrated the thin curtains in her room in a swathe of light on to her bed. She lay on her back and thought about the previous night. He had wanted to come back to her room, that Steve. She imagined Jo's face when she told her. She had to know, didn't she? She hummed to herself as she made her way to the refectory.

Breakfast was almost over when Lydia sat down heavily next to Jo. The aroma of fried food hung above the tables in an almost visible fug. No grapefruit or yoghurt today; Lydia tore off small pieces of Jo's toast and began to fiddle with her coffee spoon. She studied Jo's face from beneath her eyelids.

'How many points out of ten for Steve? I mean really.' She wrinkled her nose as Jo looked up. It was a disingenuous question.

'I wouldn't kick him out of bed, I suppose,' Jo said, looking down as she dissected her kipper. Lydia smiled into her coffee. She approved of this response but soon became coolly distant again. Jo completed her breakfast in silence.

Their fragile friendship was not really a friendship at all. Lydia suggested activities she knew would scare Jo - swimming at midnight from a famously dangerous outcrop of rocks at one end of the beach or stealing clothes from an exclusive little boutique in town. Jo resented Lydia's smirk when she hesitated. The problem was that none of her friends were as exciting as Lydia, and she was aware that she enjoyed the kudos of being seen with her. Lydia could be cruelly sarcastic, yet she possessed a charisma which drew others to her. She could steer conversations in any direction she chose with the lift of an eyebrow or a grimace. She ensured gossip was always initiated by others but was able to ridicule others under the guise of empathy. Her targets were those with a physical defect – bad skin, a speech impediment. Once, when trying unsuccessfully not to laugh at boy with severe acne, Jo had to walk away. Lydia watched her go and smiled.

That Summer, with nothing better to do, Lydia agreed to go hitching around France with Steve. Jo was not invited. She got a temp's job at the local hospital and had a brief fling with a medical student, but after the glamour of his white coat had worn off, she found his tales of the geriatric ward where he worked mind-numbingly dull. And he was always so tired that sex was infrequent and disappointing. It was a blistering hot Summer and often she sat in the hospital grounds eating her sandwiches wondering idly what Steve and Lydia were doing. Neither of them contacted her. She knew they wouldn't.

Lydia did not think about Jo. She enjoyed the sunshine and the drinking, and returned to college cheerful, relaxed and tanned. She was aware of Jo's scrutiny, and it pleased her. Steve was quiet and looked pale as if he had not been on holiday at all. Neither said much about what had happened.

A few evenings later in the noisy college bar, Steve sat alone with his pint, an open book on the table in front of him. Jo sat down but it was clear he did not want to talk. But then he looked up and said:

'Me and Lydia have called it a day.' He fiddled with the zip on his rucksack. Jo felt a guilty rush of excitement.

'Why? What's happened?'

'Oh, I dunno. France was pretty shit. My wallet was nicked, and we didn't have enough money to carry on. We ought to have come home. But she… she…' He looked at his hands. 'She was such a cow.'

Jo waited, not moving, afraid he would not go on.

'We met up with that Jack bloke – you know the one who makes those weird pots she goes on about. I think she knew he was going to be there. They started mucking around and I felt like a spare prick. She went off to some bar with him and I was really pissed off, so I went back to the hostel.'

Jo moved towards him.

'They came back at four in the morning and dear Jack just stuck with us. He is such a bastard. Arrogant, self-centred. A bit like her really. On the boat coming back she said we needed a break, and on the train from Dover she didn't say a word. Then yesterday she comes up to me, all smiles as if nothing's happened. Honestly, I've had it with her.' He paused. 'It wasn't only that. She can be such a bitch. This poor French bloke…' Steve stopped talking as others joined them at the table. Soon afterwards he stood up and left without saying goodbye.

That October was particularly wet. Lydia, sitting in her strange dark little room, watched the rain with the windows wide open. She was not thinking about Steve or Jo or anything else much. She opened a bottle of Scotch and poured some into a mug. Small gusts of wind smacked against the ill-fitting windows as they swung in the breeze.

One freezing March morning near the end of term in their final year, Lydia and Jo were walking on the beach. Lydia turned to Jo with amused resignation.

'I have nothing at all to present for my final exhibition. Not one single piece.' She lit a cigarette but appeared to be breezily unconcerned. 'We set up next week. Oh, what can I do?' She flung her hands in the air in a mocking gesture, laughing openly now.

A week later, she arrived in the car park in her old barely roadworthy VW Beetle. A box of Jack's ceramic pots sat on the back seat, with two paintings of the harbour, the work of another student at the art college, tied to the roof. Jo helped her carry them to the art studio where she arranged them in the space allocated for her work. She beamed at everyone there, and then left the building. Some marvelled at her audacity, but Jo was appalled. Lydia would have liked to have known that. She liked to appal people.

That year, Lydia rented a tiny, terraced house, a dingy place on a back street near the docks which gained notoriety because of the raucous parties and an endless supply of alcohol and drugs. It was a place in which Lydia felt comfortable, happy even, and Jo believed (incorrectly) that Lydia's contentment would somehow strengthen their friendship. For Jo, life at the little house was life on the edge. Lydia knew this. It was fun to watch her.

It was at one of these famous parties that Lydia met Steve's new room-mate Johnny, an exchange student from Bologna. He was short and stocky with thick curly black hair, an untidy beard, and heavy, brown-rimmed glasses. His expression was one of perpetual confusion, and he often looked lost, smiling uncertainly when drinks were thrust into his hand. Jo felt sorry for him.

For some reason no one, perhaps not even Lydia herself, ever understood, Lydia was intrigued by Johnny. He had a pleasant face but was neither charismatic nor wealthy, characteristics important to Lydia. This made her behaviour even more puzzling. She began to treat him like a pet dog; she stroked his hair, made him eat chocolate from her hand. It was embarrassing to watch and there was occasional nervous laughter. Johnny was good humoured and if he ever expressed any mild irritation, Lydia was spurred on to further indignities.

'Good boy Johnny,' she cried once when they were all sitting on the beach. She picked up a stick as if to throw for him to fetch. Steve, who rarely spoke to Lydia, was furious. He tried to persuade Johnny to stay away from her, but it became obvious to everyone, particularly to Lydia herself, that Johnny was obsessed with her and was willing to weather her endless mockery.

Johnny would do almost anything to please her. He stole the cheese and yoghurt she liked from the little supermarket in town, drove her around in the ancient mini he had bought, even picked her up from dates with other men. Lydia appeared to thrive on this unconditional adoration. She was not close to anyone at college, yet here was Johnny looking at her with sad brown eyes, listening to her with such devotion.

From the side-lines, Jo and Steve watched. After one particularly excruciating evening when Lydia had mocked Johnny mercilessly as he danced to the band, Steve turned to Jo and said: 'See? Look at her. Look what she's doing. It's France all over again. She's a selfish, little bitch. See what I mean now?'

Friendship and loyalty to Lydia were becoming more of a challenge for Jo. This was made worse by the knowledge that neither were of any importance to Lydia. Perhaps this made it easier for Jo to confront Lydia one afternoon when they were walking on the beach.

'Lyd, I think you're making Johnny really miserable.' Lydia stopped and turned towards Jo with narrowed eyes.

'Oh, he thinks he loves me,' she said, and paused to pick up some pebbles. 'It's all a balancing act, isn't it?' She began to throw the pebbles into the waves. 'You want to be loved, and then you can't wait to get away from those who love you.' It was the most intimate thing Jo had ever heard her say. 'And thereby lies the tension.' She smirked.

'But Johnny. Honestly?' And she turned and ran towards the promenade, her red hair streaming out behind her.

On the penultimate evening of term, Jo struggled up the road with a box of books and a bag of clothes. Steve was leaving the following day for a job interview and had agreed to take some luggage home for her. She was disappointed he was leaving early. She knew it was both unwise and pointless to investigate her feelings about that too closely.

The bar was as crowded as usual. Johnny was sitting on his own on a radiator in the bay window. He waved to Jo and moved along to make room for her.

'You look pleased with yourself.'

'I was going to leave tonight but I'm going to stay - just for the farewell dance.' He looked into his beer and then up at Jo. She did not know how to respond. The college dances had often been scenes of public humiliation for him. Why would he want to put himself through that again?

'Lydia just called round. She asked me to go with her.' Through the thick lens of his glasses, Jo could not read his expression but there was a certain sadness in the set of his mouth. He laughed in a self-deprecating way. 'So at least I can die a happy man.'

The farewell dance was poignant only because it was the final one. There was ostentatious weeping and some of the girls, overcome with emotion and alcohol, hugged each other with tearful affirmations of lifelong friendship. Lydia looked at them with disdain.

'Oh God, just look at them.' She laughed the harsh bitter laugh Jo did not like. She was wearing shabby blue dungarees, her hair caught back with a child's pink plastic comb, in startling contrast to the skimpy crepe and lace worn by the other girls.

Lydia did not want to be there and suggested they leave. A small group squeezed into two cars - Johnny's mini and Lydia's red Beetle – and drove over to West Bay, along the deserted coast road. The moon, high in the sky, was deep apricot. They didn't feel the chill as they stumbled into each other, laughing, whilst collecting pieces of driftwood which littered the beach.

Someone discovered a large tree which had fallen from the cliff above and tipped over in the sand, its roots stretching up like arms, a shower of mud clods and gravel beneath it. They managed to construct an unsteady tepee, tall enough for them all to sit beneath. Lydia's face was covered with moving shadows when she suggested they set fire to it. They scrambled out and gazed up as the wood caught in a blaze of crackling flame, shooting sparks into the night sky. The atmosphere was almost celebratory.

Some of the group began to sidle off into the dunes until only Lydia, Johnny and Jo were left by the fire. Jo began to walk towards the shoreline. She doubted Lydia would make any effort to ensure Johnny's last night was a memorable one. She sat smoking a cigarette, looking around her as if she had lost something. Johnny prodded the fire with a stick.

The sea was grey, flat, and uninviting. Jo felt no enthusiasm for a midnight swim. She was cold and miserable as she walked across the damp, shingly sand. She wanted to wallow in melancholy. The three years had gone by quickly and she felt scarred by them, but she could not explain why.

Jo turned and saw not one but two bonfires beneath the rocks, the smaller one turning around like ignited tumbleweed. She began to walk back. She could see Lydia standing up, staring at the fire, a cigarette still in her hand, a sweater drawn around her shoulders. As Jo got closer, she heard an odd wailing like an injured animal, followed by shouts. The others began to emerge from the dunes and were running to where a fire within a fire burned red and gold, flames climbing higher and higher.

Johnny lay on his back inside the collapsed wooden structure, his legs trapped beneath two of the largest branches of the tree. The flames had engulfed the flimsy red silk shirt they had watched him dance around in so often. It now lay in tattered strips across his chest like ragged streams of black blood. He was struggling to turn over so that he could crawl out. The frames of his glasses had partially melted on one side, distorting his features into a grotesque mask where only his cracked and swollen lips were recognisable. The smell of burning flesh was overpowering; just a few singed curls of black hair remained on top of his head. His trousers had melded into the wood covering his legs and that section of the fire was gaining momentum so that no-one could get anywhere near him. His arms, partially covered by smouldering embers, were moving slowly up and down, and his beloved black suede boots crackled and curled around his feet. Finally, he had no energy left to scream.

'What the hell's happened?' a voice rang out. Lydia did not move but continued to stare at the fire. In the dark it was impossible to see the expression on her face.

They ran around Johnny's body crying and shouting to each other, incapable of doing anything constructive. Someone threw a bottle of cider over him. A blanket, tossed towards him rather than over him, began to smoulder and burn. They jabbed at him ineffectively with pieces of driftwood, but it was impossible to get his body out without risking severe burns themselves. Smoke billowed across the bay drifting further and further towards the sea and it became difficult to breathe anywhere near the fire. At last, one of the girls covered her hands with a hoodie and pulled a smoking branch away from Johnny's legs. Bottles of sea water were thrown over him and he was dragged out on to the sand. Parts of his clothing were still burning but with difficulty they managed to roll him over and over into a small rock pool. The final flames hissed. He was still breathing but Jo knew it was too late. She took off her sweatshirt and laid it over him.

Someone yelled at Lydia to go and get help. She looked up as if in a dream, her eyes slightly unfocused. She brushed sand from her dungarees before walking away to where the beach met the road. She disappeared over the hill. She did not look back.

Almost an hour later a police car arrived followed by paramedics and an ambulance. Jo could not bear to look at Johnny's face although Lydia, having returned at last, stared down at him a few times. For one terrible moment Jo thought she was going to lean over and pat him. 'Good dog.' She remained silent and looked puzzled whenever anyone asked her what had happened. It was as if she really did not know.

So many questions. Most of the students were barely sober and could not help much. All of them were frightened. They were told to report to the police station the following day, but Lydia was taken to one side. She turned and stared blank-faced at Jo before being driven away in the police car. The ambulance carrying Johnny's lifeless body drove in fits and starts over the unforgiving sand.

Jo walked home. The sun struggled to lighten a stubborn grey sky. In her room she lay down, but sleep would not come. She showered away sand and the putrid smell of burning which clung to her hair. Slowly she packed the rest of her things into the same battered suitcase she had arrived with three years before. She crept out of the student halls for the last time.

Dizzy with lack of sleep and a throbbing head, Jo walked nearly a mile to the police station. She made a statement to an inspector who stared at her closely and was less than sympathetic. She provided the information he requested but her story sounded unconvincing. She agreed she would not leave the country 'in the near future' (if only) because the police would be in touch with her. It did not even occur to her to ask if Lydia was there and if she was alright.

Jo bought a coffee at the station – bitter hot water with an apologetic froth – and a stale cheese sandwich which she threw away in disgust before boarding the train. She gave up trying to read her book and sat in miserable silence, failing to leave behind the events of last night. Lydia was there all the time. She could not get Lydia's face out of her head.

The following months were a continual stream of interviews and hearings. Newspaper reports were blunt and judgemental; practically all of them suggested that Johnny's death was the result of a drug-fuelled student orgy on the beach. Jo learned from the press that Lydia had been arrested. Salacious stories appeared in news magazines with photographs of Lydia wearing the kerchief in her hair, looking thin and wan. Between the court hearings, no-one saw her; it was rumoured she had locked herself away in a flat somewhere in London. Even if she had wanted to, Jo had no idea how she might contact her.

During an interview with an indiscreet social worker, it was revealed that Lydia had been removed from her parents and put into care after setting fire to their bedroom when she was twelve. The social worker laboured the point that Lydia had shown no remorse, but even so she was allowed back home two years later. Eventually she had run away to London but little more than that was known. Jo felt unsettled at this news. Setting fire to her parents' bedroom, she thought. What irony. She did not want to see anyone else who had been there that night. Who would want to be reminded of what had happened or even of Lydia herself?

But the nightmare remained. She began to sleep badly and had to get help for her alcohol intake. She had panic attacks and wondered if these feelings of despair would ever end. The blame was put squarely on Lydia. How pleased Lydia would have been to have known, she thought.

As she sat through the trial on a sunny Autumn morning, Jo began to doubt whether she had ever really known Lydia, or whether she had ever been able to call her a friend. The courtroom was very bright and resembled a television film-set, yet as the clock ticked and lawyers rustled notes and folders, it began to feel chilly and claustrophobic.

That day, Jo learned things she ought to have known about Lydia but had never thought to ask. She was born in South Africa for a start, and her home address was given as somewhere in Hull, yet Jo remembered her dashing off to London at the end of every term.

The greatest revelation was the existence of her parents. Jo had always assumed they were dead. Hadn't Lydia told her they were? She was sure she had. But there they were, sitting in front of Jo in the public gallery, dressed in tight uncomfortable clothes. Their expressions were grim, and they did not speak to each other.

Lydia looked like her father – his wide mouth and red hair, although his was thinning and Jo suspected he lacked her charisma. He fiddled with his collar, adjusting it because it was too loose but, unlike Lydia, he tried not to draw attention to himself. He was wearing cheap white plastic trainers which glimmered incongruously beneath his trouser hems. Jo was overcome with pity for him. Lydia's mother had the face of the recipient of permanent bad news. One cheek was covered with a deep red birthmark. She sat upright as if she had a sprig of holly beneath her chin and stared straight ahead at a spot just above the coat-of-arms behind the judge. She did not look at Lydia.

Lydia spoke quietly when she gave evidence. It was a convincing performance. Her clear confident voice now had a strangled overtone. The entire public gallery sat up sharply when she claimed that Johnny had attempted to rape her.

'I pushed him away,' she said. 'He slumped backwards and fell into the fire. I tried to pull him out, I really did.' There was a break in her voice. 'But I wasn't strong enough. I just couldn't do it.'

Jo did not believe her for one minute. Lydia had been standing very still when Jo returned that night; there had been little evidence of a physical struggle to get Johnny out of the fire. But a middle-aged woman in a flowery dress on the jury was shaking her head sadly and looking at Lydia with sympathetic concern.

Jo gave evidence, aware of Lydia's eyes on her. She was not closely questioned. There was so much more she could have said but was relieved she did not have to do so.

When Lydia was given four years for manslaughter the only reaction was a slight jerk of the head from her father, and a quiet gasp in the public gallery. Lydia stared at the judge when the sentence was announced. She showed no emotion. Then, as she had done throughout the trial, she looked around the court. She may have looked at Jo. If she did, Jo did not notice. Watching Lydia's red hair swinging around her face as she walked down the steps behind the dock, Jo doubted she would ever see her again.

Journey to Matonga to Dance

Catherine is a Good Woman. Today she has purchased *The Big Issue* from the Iranian man with the limp and the sad eyes outside Marks and has bought coffee and a doughnut for every third homeless person she has passed on the street. More than that and she would never have got to the telephone helpline where she listens to the despairing and the suicidal once a week. She is often frustrated that it is company policy not to offer advice. She feels she could do so much more if that were not the case; she is undoubtedly a problem solver.

Hardly aware of it, or at least unwilling to recognise it for what it is, charitable deeds fill an empty void in Catherine's life. She smiles a great deal, stretching her lips across strong white teeth, her face a perpetual study of empathy. Helping the homeless produces a warm glow of self-satisfaction which Catherine mistakes for affection, gratitude, and a dependence on her from those to whom she gives. Sometimes she can convince herself that *this* is what she has been searching for, that this is something which gives her life some purpose. She almost sees herself as Catherine the Benevolent and craves the recognition from others when they hear about the good work she is doing.

Her mother's Knitting Circle, their soft lumpy bodies sinking ever deeper into their soft lumpy armchairs, wind wool around trembling up-stretched hands and listen to her stories. She appreciates this captive audience who, if they are not listening to her, at least nod in appreciation.

'I don't think they've had a decent meal in weeks,' she says of those homeless people fortunate enough to have been helped by her. 'Thank God I come along at just the right moment. It's only a cup of coffee but I'm sure it means the world to them.' The bland platitudes cause their old eyes to water with admiration. But Catherine knows that when she is talking to her younger sister's Stitch and Bitch group, they are less sentimental and less patient with her tales.

Her life changes when she sees a job advertised in a Sunday paper – charitable work, volunteering in Africa. How sweet it sounds! Her reaction is almost physical, and she has to sit down. She reads the advertisement several times, her heart thumping pleasantly. It is the very pinnacle of all she holds dear. Here is her chance to show the world what a Good Woman can do. In a typically spontaneous gesture, she volunteers for a six-month placement at a college in Northern Uganda, in a town so remote she cannot find it on the map. With shining eyes, she speaks to her sister Rowena about parched lands, malnourished babies, ill-equipped schools, all desperate for help, specifically hers. She describes the ineffectiveness of missionaries striding through the jungle waving their Bibles, anathema to Catherine; she is a practical person and has no time for Christian do-gooders. She talks of being welcomed at the airport by tribal dancers and laughing crowds who will place leafy garlands around her neck.

At various times during the day that Catherine leaves England for Kampala, Rowena pauses at her desk at work and wonders precisely where Catherine is at that moment. She knows Catherine will be equally vague about this and smiles fondly. Poor Catherine.

Kampala airport is small, dirty, and chaotic. Dull lights shine down on queues of anxious faces, putting a surreal gloss on the scene as if everyone is moving backwards and forwards underwater. Catherine is tired and confused as she pushes through the crowds towards the exit. It is hot and steamy outside. Swarms of mosquitoes fly directly from the swamps of Lake Victoria and dance around her. She can feel the pinpricks of their cruel little bites on her ankles and the top of her head. She thinks she may be falling asleep standing up.

A young white man materialises from the boiling crowd, waving his arm high above the bobbing heads. He is carrying a card with her name on it, incorrectly spelt. There are damp patches under his arms and his thin legs protrude from over-large cargo shorts.

'Catherine?' he shouts. 'Nick Hammond. This way.' He does not wait for a reply but strides ahead. Dragging her cases which he does not offer to help her with, Catherine follows him to an open area where a large dusty bus stands waiting. It is surrounded by people jostling each other, pushing suitcases, flapping boxes, and a mass of other unidentifiable luggage into an open compartment at the side.

Nick Hammond turns to her and grins. Africa may not be the best location for his good works, she thinks. His face is very red and bears the angry scars of insect bites. He is perspiring heavily, and his bodily aroma is pungent. Perhaps you can't buy deodorant here? she thinks. She stands back while he struggles to pack her luggage into the bus. Sweating more profusely than ever he turns back to her.

'Welcome to Uganda,' he says. 'Good journey?' She nods. He looks around him. 'I'm afraid your luggage is likely to arrive before you do.' Catherine wonders what on earth he means by that. She turns towards the bus. Emblazoned across the front windscreen in gold letters are the words 'God Only Knows.' The Knitting Circle would have been pleased to see this.

'Should I get on?' she says.

'No, I've arranged other transport. Wait here.' She watches Nick disappear into the crowd as the bus carrying her luggage suddenly roars away in clouds of dust and diesel fumes. Nick returns on the back of a motorbike. He gets off and money passes hands. A dirty crash helmet is passed over to her and

Catherine swallows hard. Surely this isn't…? Nick tries to help her on to the bike and after the third attempt she manages to swing her leg over the pillion seat. She thanks God she is wearing trousers and remembers her mother's words: 'Best wear slacks. So much comfier to travel in.' She is fairly certain this mode of transport is not what her mother had in mind.

Nick waves goodbye and disappears again. The driver on the motor bike stares straight ahead. The bike jolts into life and they shoot ahead, trapped in a stream of traffic moving away from the airport on to an uneven road. Surrounded by more bikes carrying branches of bananas, cages of chickens, whole families, and even live goats strapped to the side, Catherine tries to focus on the roadside shacks and the people wandering past, but eventually finds closing her eyes is by far the best option. She has never felt so uncomfortable or unsafe in her life. She expects to fall into the road in front of oncoming trucks at any moment.

Soon afterwards the road becomes little more than a wide yellow track encrusted with rocks and pebbles. Far from the dry dusty plain she had imagined, this is a land of green hills strewn with vast boulders and lush vegetation. Swathes of bush surround villages of grass-roofed huts and neatly farmed smallholdings. Women walk along orange and yellow murram roads, balancing water pots, wide fruit baskets or massive branches on their heads. There are children everywhere, walking, on bikes, by the roadside, waving as they pass. Catherine raises a tentative arm once or twice only to grab on to the bike again as quickly as possible.

She loses all track of time. Her limbs are completely numb, and her face lies buried beneath a thick layer of red dust. A hot breeze does not refresh but raises the temperature as they travel further north. At a roadside market, crowds appear from nowhere, thrusting pineapples, bottled water, bananas, and gristly kebabs into her face. Her entire body is vibrating but the stop brings some relief before the journey begins again.

Crashing over a craggy boulder and dipping deep into a waterlogged rut finally rouses Catherine from a nauseous half-slumber. She has survived the journey by swallowing a whole packet of travel sickness pills and half a box of Bourbon biscuits. They have cancelled themselves out and twice she has been sick on the red earth road, on one occasion observed from above by a solemn female baboon suckling her baby. They stop for Catherine to use a village pit latrine. She stares down the deep hole into hell itself. She had always believed that nothing could be worse than a Glastonbury Portaloo. Except this is. It really is.

Finally, when Catherine is barely conscious, they stop. She staggers from the motor bike and stands in front of a row of tiny mud brick houses with tin roofs. Nick Hammond is there (quite how, she cannot fathom.) Her luggage has also mysteriously appeared and lies in an untidy heap on the ground. Nick removes a key from his pocket and says in an offhand voice: 'This is your house.' A small crowd mills around in the muddy lane next to a field of skinny goats and chickens.

'Hallo,' Catherine says with as much enthusiasm as she can muster. 'Hujambo.' This is the only Swahili word the charity has provided in their booklet 'Useful Tips for Your New Life in Uganda!' which she has flicked through on the plane. Her greeting is met with incomprehension. The children hide in the folds of their mothers' skirts, and the adults are stony-faced. Catherine had expected to be warmly welcomed by villagers grateful for her presence. She had envisaged attractive little huts surrounding an open fire where she would talk with the women as they cooked together, and the men would whittle twigs into simple household tools, singing African folk songs as they worked. At dusk, she would go with the women to the well with a clay pot on her head, and then they would sit combing each other's hair as they told stories and recited poetry. She had not realised that few would be able to speak any English at all or, as she discovered later, that carrying a heavy water pot on your head was not a skill she possessed.

She smells cooking and sees mud ovens in front of each house, uncomfortably close to more pit latrines. Inside her house she climbs over a broken rattan sofa to a small metal table and two chairs. A cracked sink produces a trickle of brown water. Two gas rings balance precariously on top of a metal gas bottle. A second room contains a grubby mattress with a torn mosquito net hanging limply from the ceiling. Catherine thinks that catching malaria is the least of her problems.

The heat washes through glassless windows. There is a sweet unpleasant smell which later becomes familiar - bat droppings. Catherine realises she has been holding her breath for some time.

The Ugandan sun slides behind the Congolese hills in the distance. She becomes aware of a woman behind her, silently offering a blue plastic beaker of black tea. She takes it from her just as hundreds of flapping bats leave the trees and darken the sky, setting out to find their supper.

Catherine does not sleep well. Rats scratch about on the roof, and she braces herself for one to fall on top of her at any minute. She wakes to a blinding light and three small faces peering through the window. Two rusty nails protrude crookedly from each side of the frame, and she drapes a towel across them. This does not provide much privacy.

She feels more optimistic today. Unwashed (the trickle of water has dried up completely), she follows a river of people walking along a track towards a collection of brightly coloured shacks and some ramshackle shops. The heavy beat of loud music and some unfamiliar smells lead her to a large market. It is not as chaotic as it first appears. Beans, potatoes, tomatoes, avocados, ground nuts and the ubiquitous bananas lie on woven mats on the ground, goats and chickens wandering around between them. Printed cloth and cheap blue soap are piled up on old tables around the edge, and behind them rows and rows of sewing machinists produce cotton shirts, trousers, and dresses.

Perspiring more than she would have thought possible, Catherine feels weak as she looks around. People stare at her curiously. Stalls by the roadside sell black tea, and sweet yellow bread. Vegetables simmer in rusting metal pans. She sits down awkwardly on a plastic stool at one of them and points to the tea bubbling in a large saucepan. She is convinced the women are laughing at her discomfiture, and she does not know what to say to them.

The people around her are poor - Catherine can see that. But they are not starving, and they do not appear to be unhappy with their lot. As far as she can tell, the local economy in the market appears to work efficiently. She watches the bargaining and laughter during every transaction as fruit and vegetables change hands and recognises a sense of community as people greet each other with a formal handshake followed by a long conversation. She cannot see any beggars, and this makes her feel oddly surplus to need. She tells herself that she will soon find a place where she will be both needed and appreciated, but that may not be here in the town perhaps.

The sounds around her meld into one great noise so that even her little tin-roofed house seems appealing. She is exhausted and, now in the heat of the day, she begins the long trudge home.

Catherine is shown to a tiny classroom at the college the following day. On a crumbling wall is a barely usable chalkboard, and in front of that stand four wooden tables and some battered chairs. Twelve young students - all boys - suddenly arrive together. They stand perfectly still, and stare at her.

'Hallo,' says Catherine. 'I'm Catherine.' They repeat her name in unison twice. She invites them to sit by pointing at the chairs and begins to talk, slowly.

She has never been trained to teach English. Most of the students understand 'hallo' and 'goodbye' and quickly pick up 'my name is…' But the simple games and rhymes she remembers from her childhood which she written down in her notebook make no sense to them at all. It is just when she is beginning to despair that she introduces 'I Spy.' They understand the concept of the game at once (unlike 'My Grandmother went to Market' which has not been an unqualified success), and repeat 'with my little eye' over and over as though it is the funniest thing they have ever heard. They would play it all day if they could Catherine thinks, and in the following weeks calls of 'with my little eye' follow her as she walks across the dilapidated campus. In class, without prompting, they repeat certain phrases which they seem to think are important, several times. 'Do you understand?', 'we understand', 'that is good,' 'I come from England', 'I am a Ugandan boy', 'I like beans. Do you like beans?' Catherine is disconcerted by this at first but gradually understands that repetition is a key ingredient of the way they learn. They begin to teach her new words too which she also repeats, and they are delighted with her, clapping and whooping encouragement.

Their English remains poor however, and it is not always easy. Catherine perseveres. She begins to think of them as 'her students' and can see they are keen to learn. At the end of the lesson, they begin to crowd around her, hoping this will encourage her to carry on talking. With some post-its she has brought with her from England, and which they regard with interest, she sticks name labels on to their shirts and wears one herself. They wear them every day even when they become torn and grubby, and she has run out of replacements. She works hard to remember their names and eventually, despite initial reticence, she learns more about their lives, the homes they have come from. They talk about the vegetables they grow, the hens and goats they keep, the fish they catch in the rivers nearby. They want to know what vegetables she grows in England and are incredulous when she says she does not grow any. She talks to them about Manchester United and Arsenal, football teams they support with such enthusiasm. They have no idea that that these teams are based in England. Their spoken English slowly improves.

At the end of class one afternoon, she collects together the frugal teaching aids she has made for them and stacks up the chairs. Believing herself to be alone and unaware that the students are watching her through a small window, her floor sweeping evolves into a kind of ballet as she moves from one end of the room to the other, her body twisting slowly and gracefully as she sings a Ugandan song they have taught her. She props the broom against the wall and continues to dance, raising her arms above her head and spinning round. She becomes giddy and laughs at herself as the dance comes to an end. But as she walks home through the bean field and passes the children collecting water in large yellow plastic bottles, she is aware of a feeling of satisfied contentment. She thinks of the Knitting Circle and the Stitch and Bitch group, and how impressed they would be to see her here. It is a new sensation, not one she has felt since being in Uganda. Today she feels she had made a real difference.

Before long Catherine realises that the students regard her as the source of the only thing they really want. They have seen her use the small IPad she has brought with her and have watched American films on the street outside the barber's shop. From these snippets of evidence, they have drawn the conclusion that being able to use a laptop computer is the epitome of what being 'educated' is all about. It will get them a job in the Kampala or even Kenya if they have this technological knowledge. It will be a passport out of farming, out of the lives of poverty many of them have come from. Catherine can surely help them reach their goal, can't she? Catherine feels helpless and disheartened. She knows that the chances of acquiring laptops for her young students are minimal. But swept along by her new-found zeal, she begins to wonder if the situation is as hopeless as it appears to be. She contacts Rowena who has always prided herself on her efficiency and effectiveness. Maybe? Perhaps? Who knows?

Catherine's life is a lonely one. She spends the evenings reading one of the few books she has brought with her by the light of a precious candle and eating eggs and bread. The villagers and even her close neighbours are wary; she is a Muzungo and in their experience white people are often not to be trusted. She is alone, free to do what she likes with no man living in her house. She does not attend church. She is a stranger in their community. Catherine is beginning to understand how that feels.

Catherine would like to communicate with the local community but there has rarely been a response to her greeting of 'Hujambo.' Even when she says it to the students, they smile and look down, embarrassed. One morning she decides to tackle this problem head on and asks them about it. They explain (almost with some relief) that the word for 'hallo' is not 'Hujambo' but just 'Jambo' with an emphasis on the first syllable. Tentatively, Catherine tries this out on everyone she meets, and slowly things begin to change. Well, they smile back at least so something must be working. Gradually, combined with much miming and laughter, she can make herself partially understood.

During her early days in Matonga, Catherine would regularly count the sacrifices she had made to be there - leaving her job and her flat, eating what and when she liked, going to the cinema - and she used these as measures of the good work she was doing now. But it has slowly dawned on her that it is really the other way round. She is gaining far more from this experience than anyone is gaining from her. The reciprocal learning between herself and the students fills her with genuine pleasure. They have opened her eyes to a completely different way of living. They help her with Swahili and take delight in her successes with this. She is well-known in the market. When she visits, the women on the stalls patiently help her choose what she wants, describing their goods and miming how to cook them. You don't get that in Sainsbury's Catherine thinks. Her tiny London flat and undemanding office job feel stifling and drab. She is not much looking forward to returning home.

One morning Catherine goes to Nick's office. She has not seen him since her arrival. He is sitting by the window talking on his mobile and points to a chair, making no effort to curtail the call. Finally he turns towards her.

'Catherine. How's it going?' he says. 'Sorry I haven't been around. I've been backwards and forwards to Kampala. Thank God the airport's so close.' He stops, suddenly aware he has given something away. Catherine has not been aware of a local airport; flying to Matonga sounds a much better option than riding there on the back of a motor bike. What a bastard she thinks, putting me through that. But she has other things on her mind. She must pick her battles, and this cannot be one of them.

'I'll look forward to returning to Kampala by plane,' is all she says. His smile is polite.

'The teaching's going very well.' He interrupts her quickly.

'I've heard you're doing brilliantly. The principal says -' Catherine laughs shortly.

'I don't know how the principal knows that. I've never even met him.' There is a brief pause.

'I wanted to talk to you about the money,' says Catherine.

'The money?' Nick puts his mobile on the table.

'The £8000. The charity told me about it before I left.' She takes a creased envelope from her bag. Inside is her Useful Tips booklet and another letter addressed to her from the charity's Chair. She passes it to Nick. He begins reading and frowns. Then his face clears.

'Oh yes. The £8000. It's in the college coffers. Don't worry about it. There're loads of things we can do with that kind of money. I've already got some ideas…'

Catherine does not like his dismissive tone. In fact, she decides, she does not like him much either.

'But I had to submit a plan to the Board about how it would be spent. I've got to write a report about it when I get back. It's a condition of my placement.' She holds out her hands as if, regretfully, there is nothing she can do about it.

Nick sits very still looking out of the open door.

'Absolutely right. And what's in your plan?'

'Well, it's mainly about buying specific resources to support the students with their English and to help cover their college fees. I brought some teaching materials and books with me but what they really want are laptops.' Nick leans forward with a gentle smirk, preparing to protest. Catherine raises her hand palm outwards, and smiles.

'I know, I know,' she says. 'Electricity. Or lack of. But the library has power for some of the day. I've already looked into it. They could be used in there.'

'You wouldn't be able to afford much with that money. Drop in the ocean.' Nick speaks to her as if she is a slow child.

'I've done my homework Nick!' She does not even try to keep the triumph out of her voice. 'I've found several companies in England who provide reconditioned laptops for a fraction of the price of new ones so long as they go to a bona fide charity. Anywhere in the world. They'll even ship them over… I know!' She feigns amazement and thanks God for Rowena's diligence. 'I thought it was bit of a longshot myself, but I've checked it all out and we're ready to go.'

Nick stretches his fingers out on top of the desk and looks down at them.

'That's great Catherine. Give me the details and I'll get on to it.' He looks at her apologetically. 'Look, I'm sorry, but I need to get this done.' He points to some plans on his desk. 'So, I'm going to have to kick you out!' Catherine nods. She stands and walks to the door. She turns back to say:

'Oh, nearly forgot. Those big cooking pots in the college kitchen – they're falling apart. Could we replace them? I've seen cauldrons on sale in the market. That would sort of fit into my plan, wouldn't it?'

'Your plan. Goodness Catherine, you *are* keen.' Nick looks at her with dislike. 'Leave it with me.'

Her final weeks at the college pass more quickly than she would have liked. She enjoys her own company (who would have known?) She has made curtains for her little house out of pieces of local cloth, roughly sewing them together with more enthusiasm than skill, but nevertheless taking a disproportionate pride in the result. She has even got used to the lack of water and electricity. Like her neighbours, she plans her life around this, collecting water from the stream and building up a store of candles.

Nick says that the laptops are due to arrive two days before she leaves Matonga. Catherine goes to wait in a small field near the college where magnificent Ankole cattle graze. It is a bucolic scene were it not for the shadow of the abattoir lying in wait on the other side. Who wouldn't be soothed by this place though, surrounded by hazy-green hills and the Nile flowing so close by? she thinks. She sets off to meet the bus from Kampala, but the laptops are not aboard. She decides to wait for the next one.

On the day of her departure, Catherine walks through the field to find Nick. She has seen him dawdling along towards the campus and knows she may miss him if she does not go now. He is not in his office, but she can see him sitting with a group of college tutors under the large mango tree in the centre of the compound. He is passing something round but when he sees her approach, he attempts to collect in whatever this is.

It is too late. Catherine smiles as she sits down on one of the plastic chairs. The tutor next to her is called Adorable although she has always found him to be anything but. She feels awkward using his name. 'Good morning, Adorable,' or 'Can you help me Adorable?' Nick has no such inhibitions.

'Pass it here, Adorable,' he says. But Catherine has already seen the photo of a detached brick house, sitting in its own grounds with a distant view of Lake Victoria.

'Nick has finished building his new house,' Adorable says to her as he passes the photo back to Nick. 'It has a basin to wash inside the house with gold taps!' The others are listening and smile incredulously, raising their hands as if in worship.

'And a room for the escari on the edge of the land!'

'And chickens and goats and maybe even a cow!'

The excitement has almost reached fever pitch. Catherine thinks of the simple shacks, no bigger than her own, where the tutors live, often with their wives and children. She thinks of the pit latrines shared by several families, and wonders at Nick's boastfulness and lack of tact.

Suddenly he looks up and she meets his gaze, holding it steadily until he looks away. Clearly no expense has been spared for Nick's new house. He has the grace to look down at the ground uncomfortably.

Catherine returns to the top of the track leading away from the college where her luggage is waiting. The students are lined up and watch her in silence. Each one shakes her hand solemnly before she struggles on to the bus which has now arrived, and growls impatiently by the roadside. As the long journey south begins, she feels emotional and miserable. Her work is unfinished and now she is going home. The students will continue to sleep in dormitories riddled with mosquitoes. The promised laptops will never arrive. The cooking pots will not be replaced. The Knitting Circle and the Stitch and Bitch Group will probably have no time for her now. She has been such a fool and a powerless one at that.

Arriving in Kampala, Catherine drags her suitcases from the side of the bus. She wheels them unsteadily through swirls of red dust across the gravel track to the entrance of the airport. She has dozed on the bus journey, preventing a final glimpse of those places which have become familiar to her - the entrance to the National Park where elephants lumber across the road in massive grey gangs, the boiling waters of the Nile crashing beneath the bridge at the Pakwatch crossing, women viciously scrubbing clothes across flat stones on the banks of a stream near Matonga.

Inside the airport, not much has changed since her arrival six months before. She recognises the same security man hovering importantly near the door, his ill-fitting uniform and general officiousness apparently an integral part of the job. The air is thick with chaos and heat, trapped beneath the roof of the shabby departure hall. It is difficult to differentiate between those who are welcoming new arrivals, and those who are embarking. Family groups block gangways, delaying anxious passengers as they hurry towards check-in counters. Some pull luggage encased in heavy plastic wrapping, and others struggle with large cardboard boxes swathed in rolls and rolls of brown sticky tape.

The atmosphere is heavy and steamy. Catherine is weary and it takes her some time to acclimatise to the heady environment. She goes to the only coffee shop, where people spill out on to the concourse holding cardboard cups of coffee like trophies. Catherine cannot face coffee or perhaps she cannot face the snaking queue. She decides to check-in and wait for her flight to be called.

She hesitates. She is drawn towards the grimy window with its view outside of makeshift stalls selling bottled water and dry yellow cakes, and boda riders hanging around waiting for a fare. And always, always, she sees the tangle of thick vegetation pushing up towards the light through every available space however small, and the grey green hills in the distance.

With nowhere else to sit, she balances herself on her suitcase. And she weeps.

Suddenly she sits up very straight and places her feet firmly on the floor. She is not crying for unfulfilled ambition. She is crying because she is leaving behind the one place where she has felt comfortable in her own skin, happy even. Where what she received is so much greater than what she has given. How can she abandon that?

Through the window she can still see the bus which has brought her on the ten-hour journey from Matonga to the airport. *Jesus is my Saviour* is emblazoned in large letters above the windshield as it stands there, puffing like a wheezing hippo. Diesel fumes fill the air and passengers run around, struggling with their luggage, and grabbing children and live animals before they board.

Catherine wheels her suitcases back through the crowd to the airport's main entrance and outside towards the bus. Her luggage is grabbed by the driver and stacked into the side compartment. It is almost as though he has been expecting her. She climbs inside and finds a seat next to a woman clutching a live chicken in an inadequate woven basket, fanning herself with the hem of her dress. They smile at each other. With a grunt and a screech of tyres, the bus lumbers out of the airport.

Available worldwide from Amazon

Michael Terence
Publishing

www.mtp.agency

mtp.agency

@mtp_agency

Printed in Great Britain
by Amazon

41210568R00078